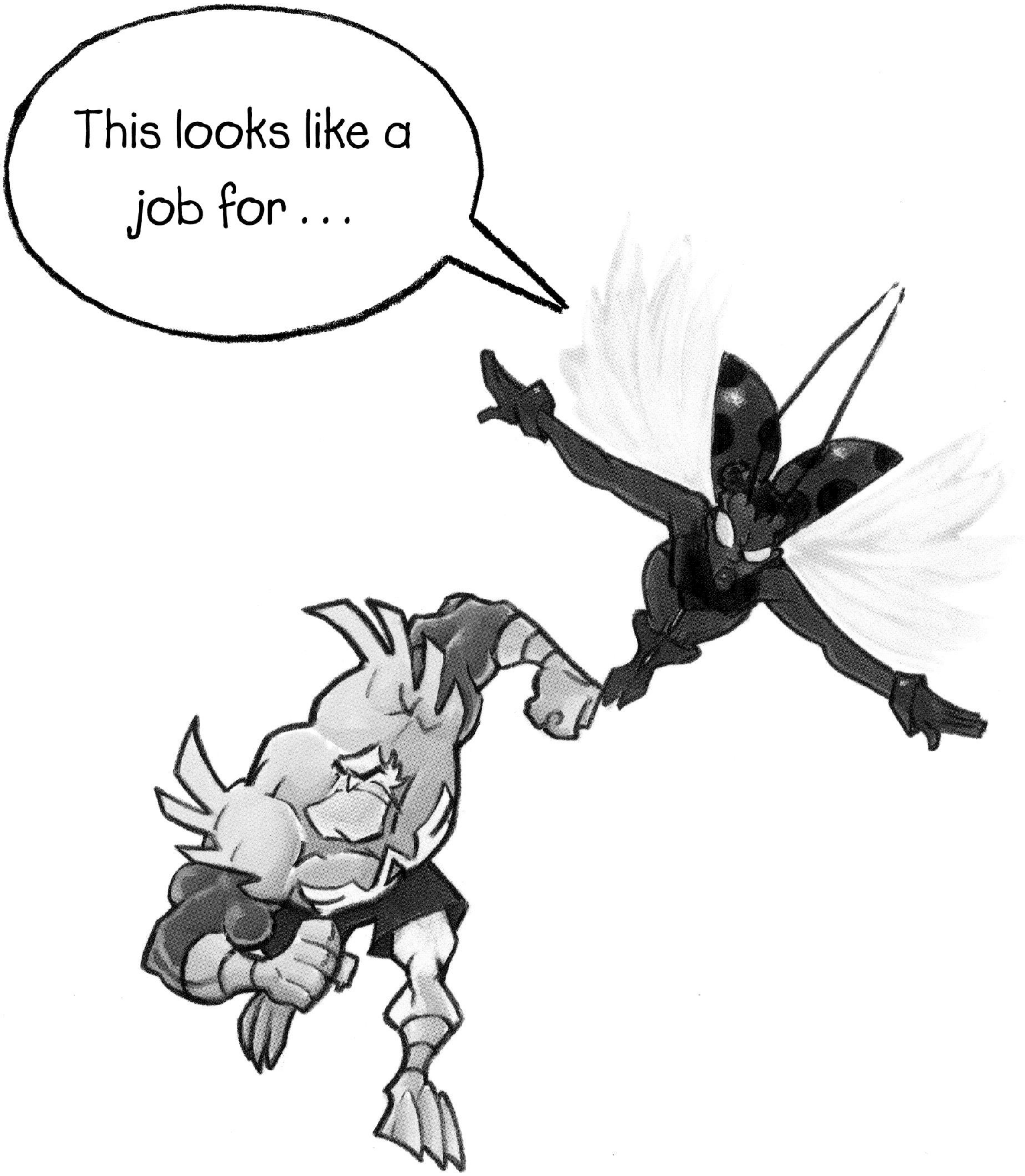
This looks like a job for . . .

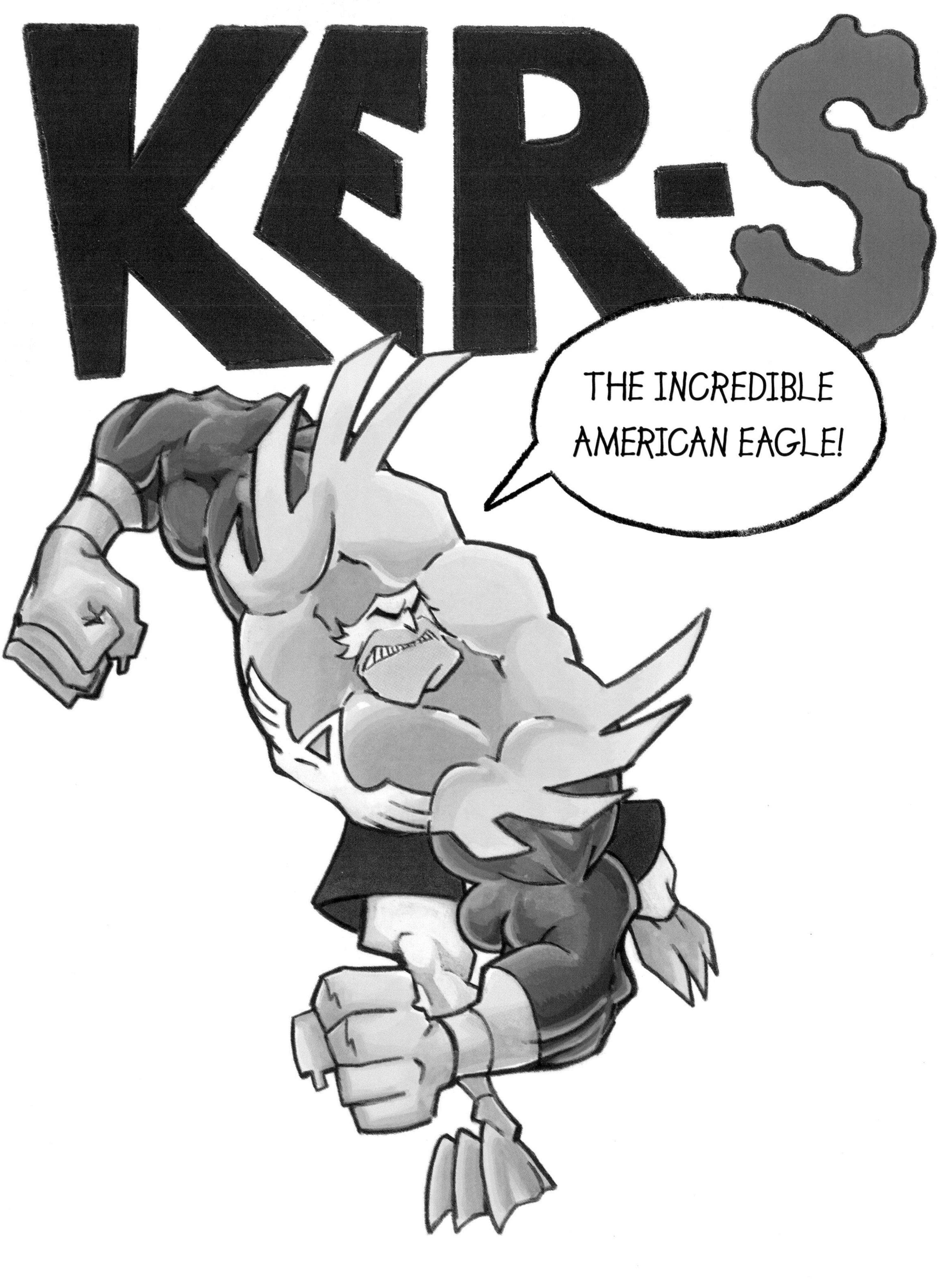
KER-$
THE INCREDIBLE AMERICAN EAGLE!

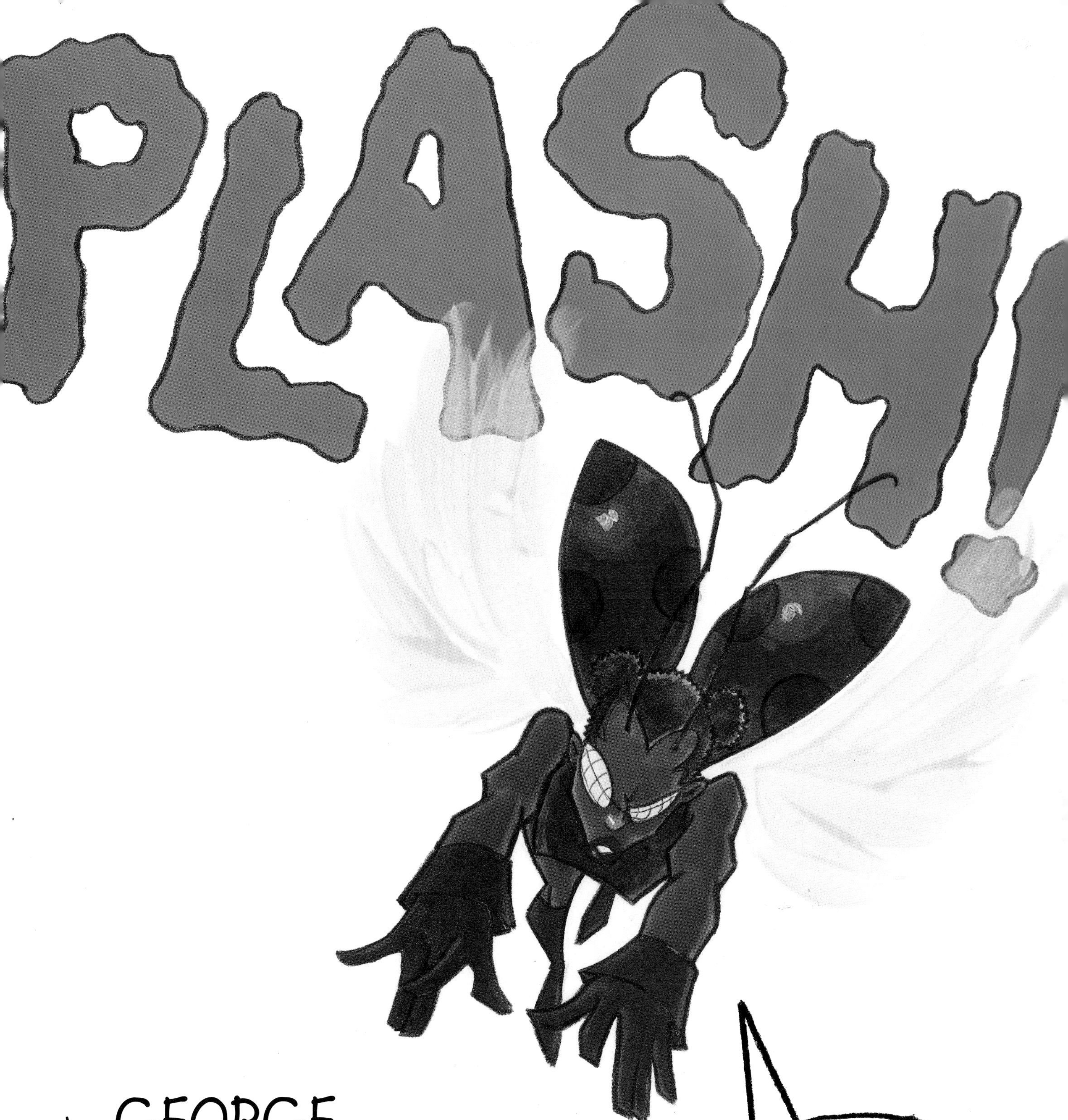
PLASH!

by GEORGE
O'CONNOR

AND
THE AMAZING
BUG LADY!

Simon & Schuster Books for Young Readers
New York London Toronto Sydney

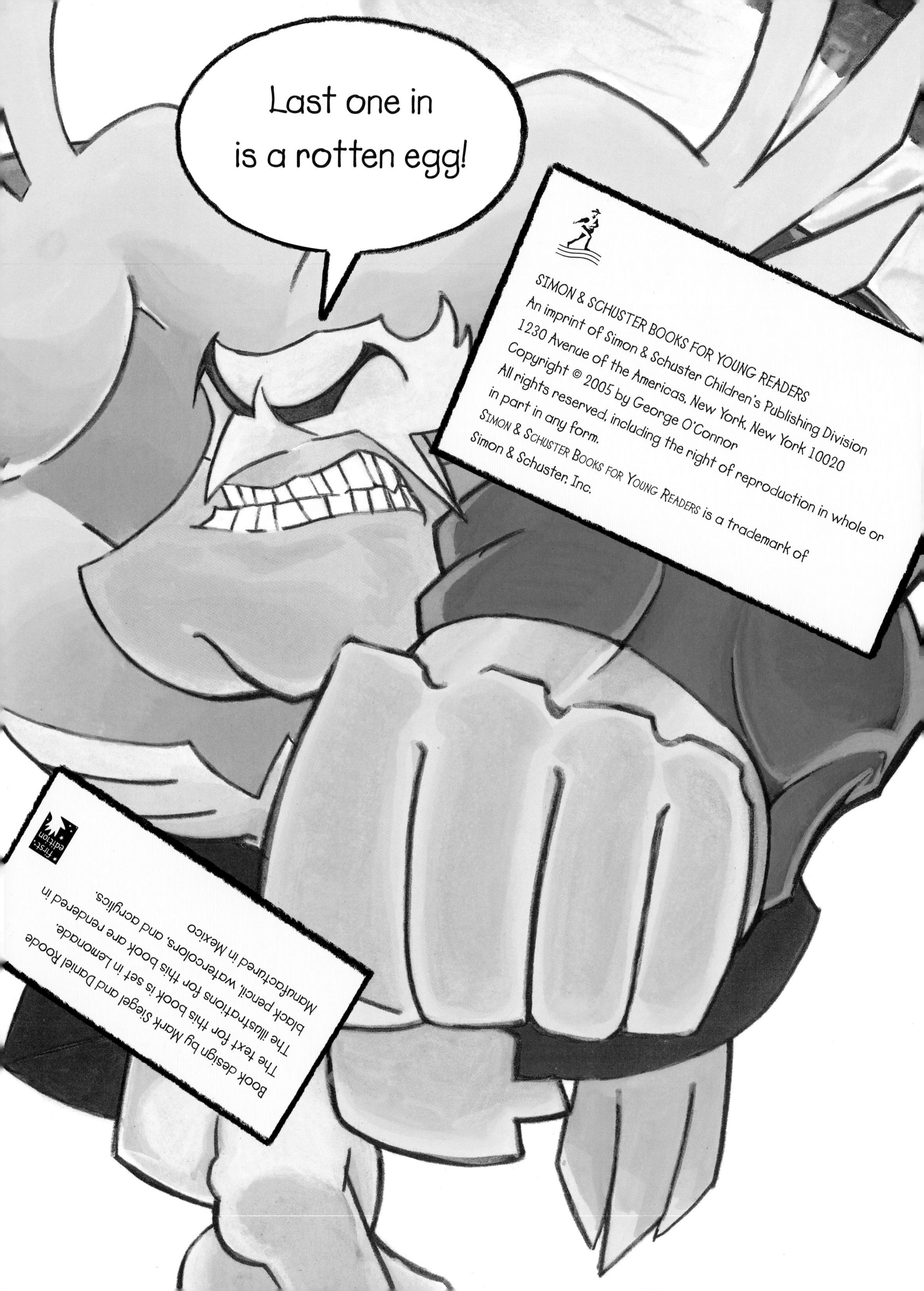
Last one in
is a rotten egg!

SIMON & SCHUSTER BOOKS FOR YOUNG READERS
An imprint of Simon & Schuster Children's Publishing Division
1230 Avenue of the Americas, New York, New York 10020

Book design by Mark Siegel and Daniel Roode
The text for this book is set in Lemonade.
The illustrations for this book are rendered in black pencil, watercolors, and acrylics.
Manufactured in Mexico
first edition

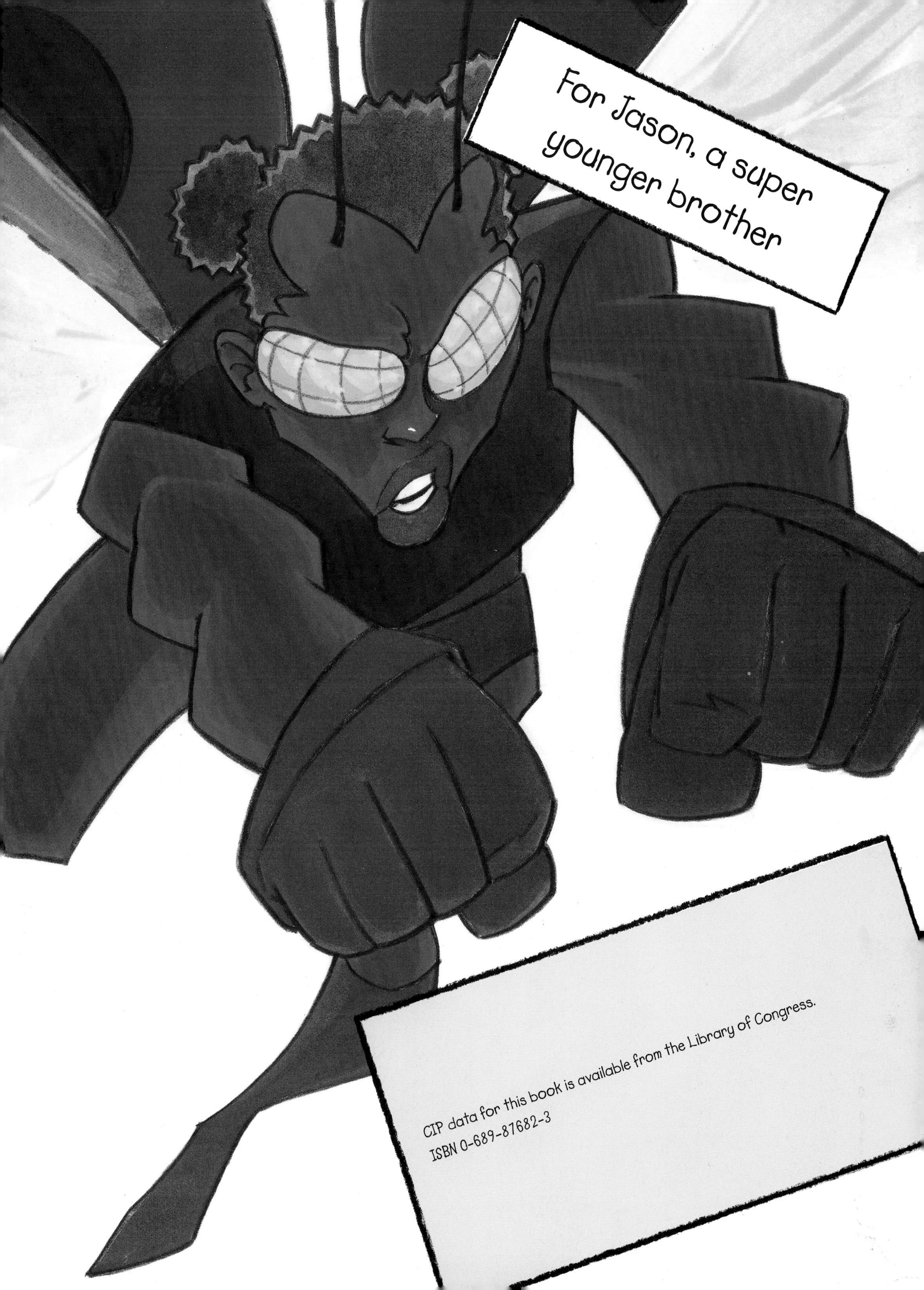

For Jason, a super younger brother

CIP data for this book is available from the Library of Congress.
ISBN 0-689-87682-3

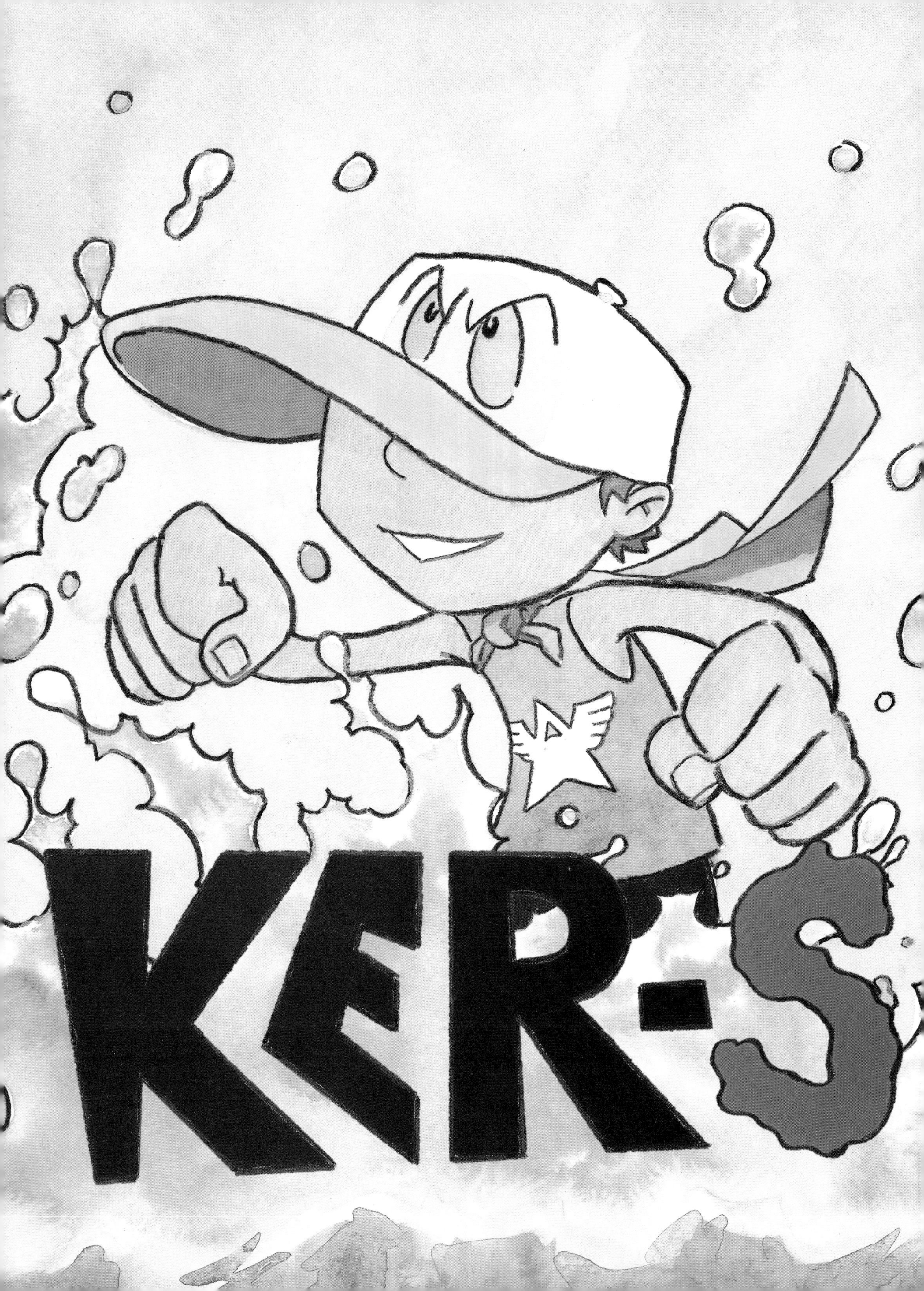
KER-S

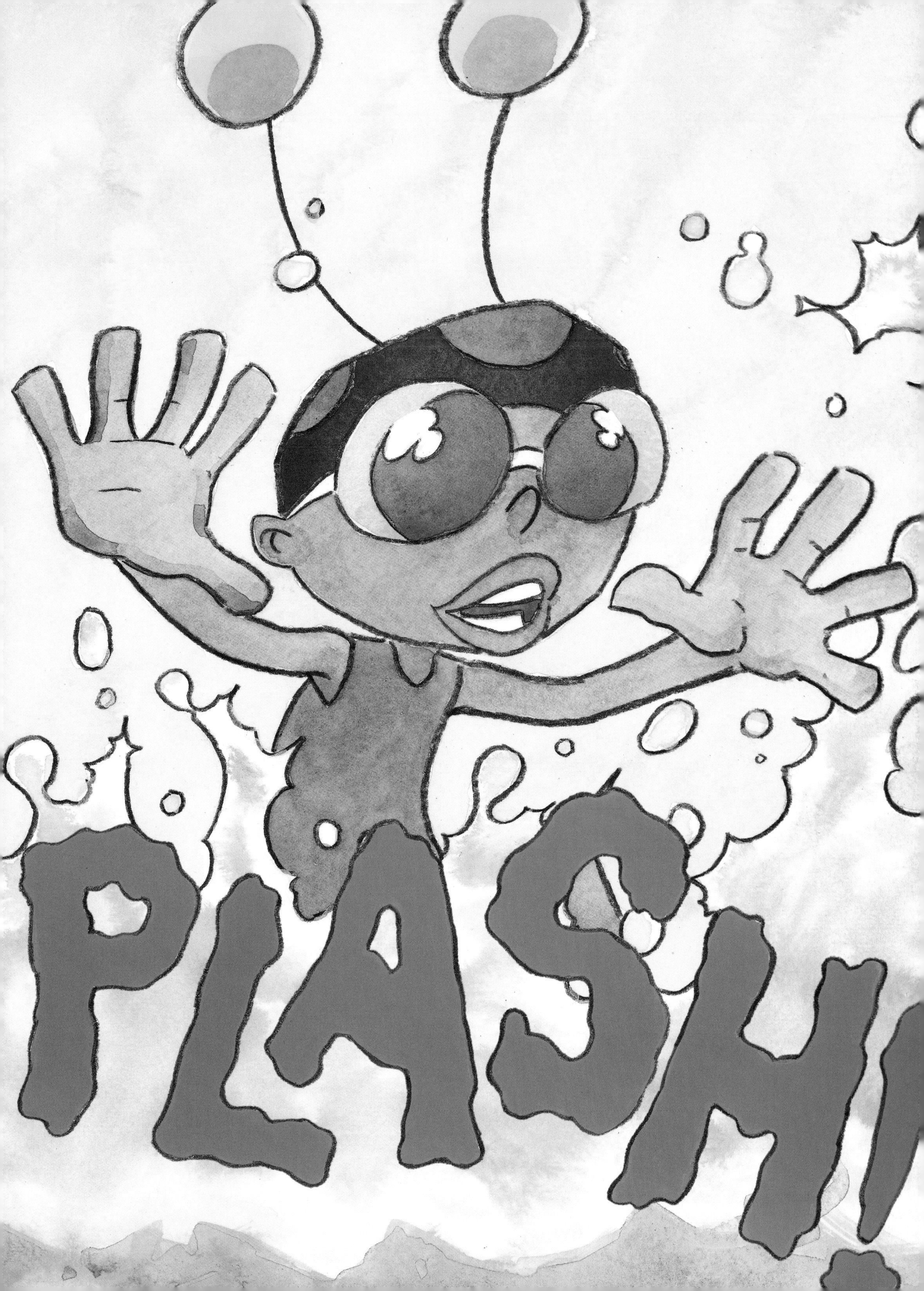
PLASH!

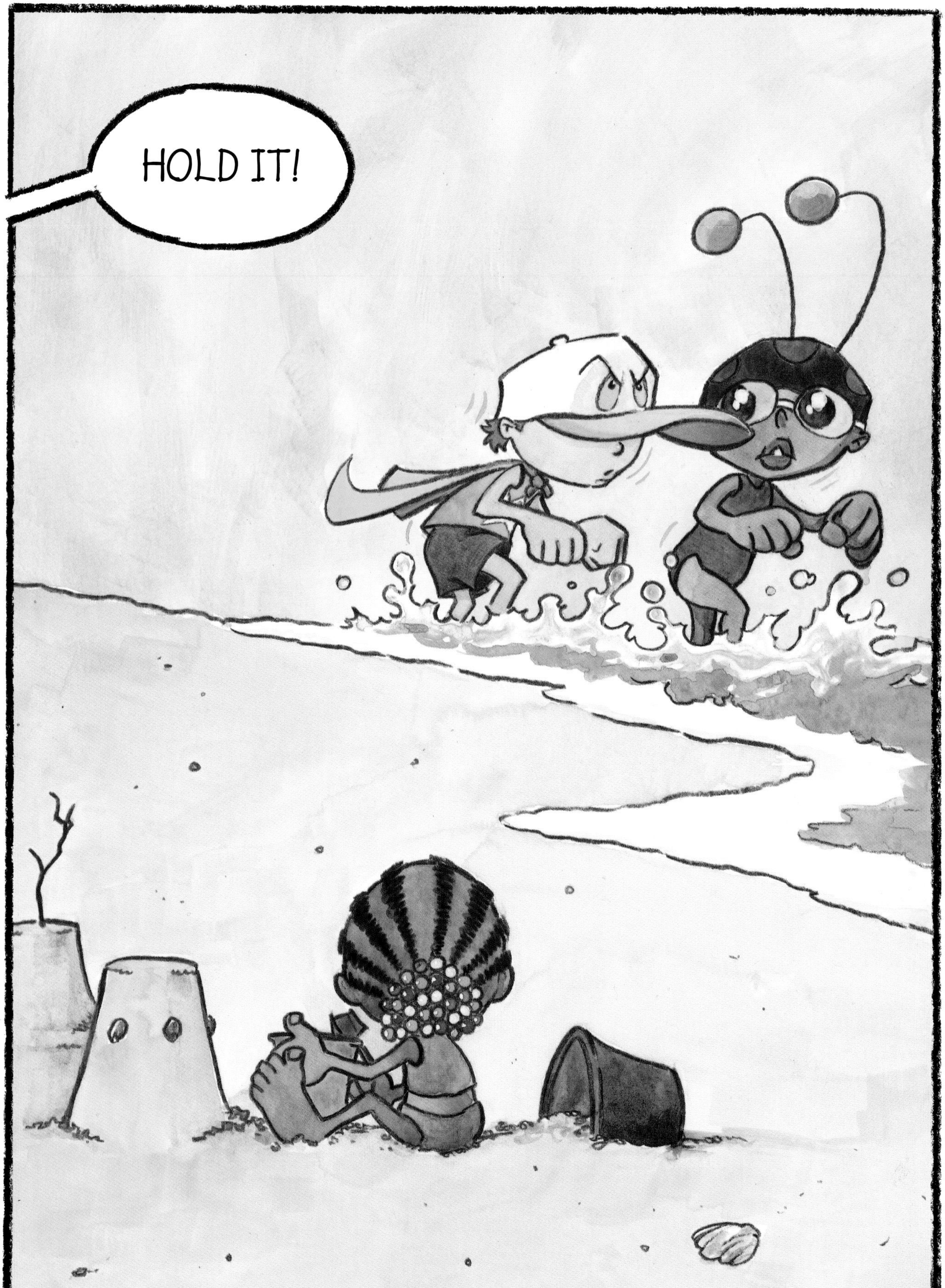
HOLD IT!

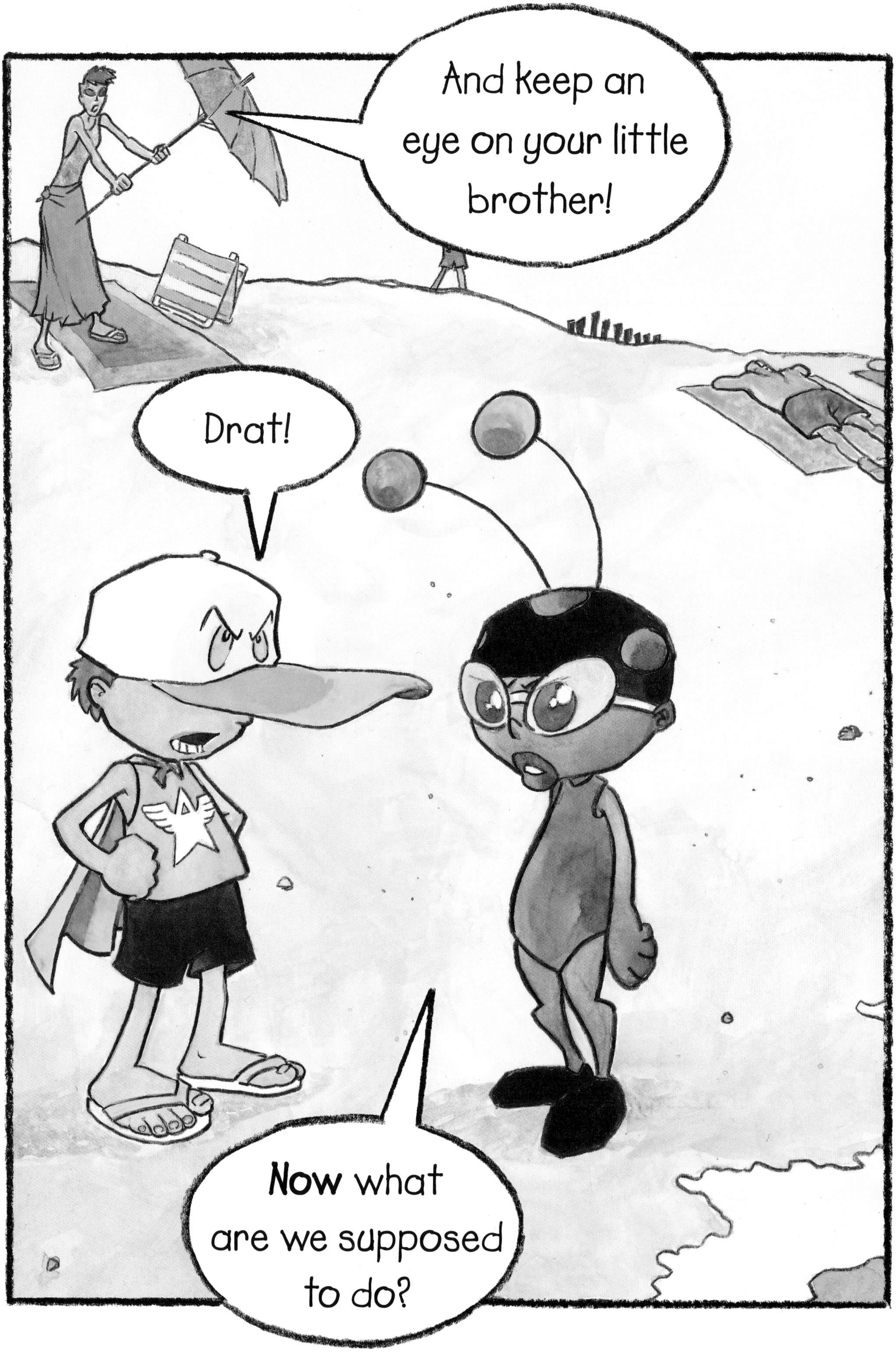
And keep an eye on your little brother!
Drat!
Now what are we supposed to do?

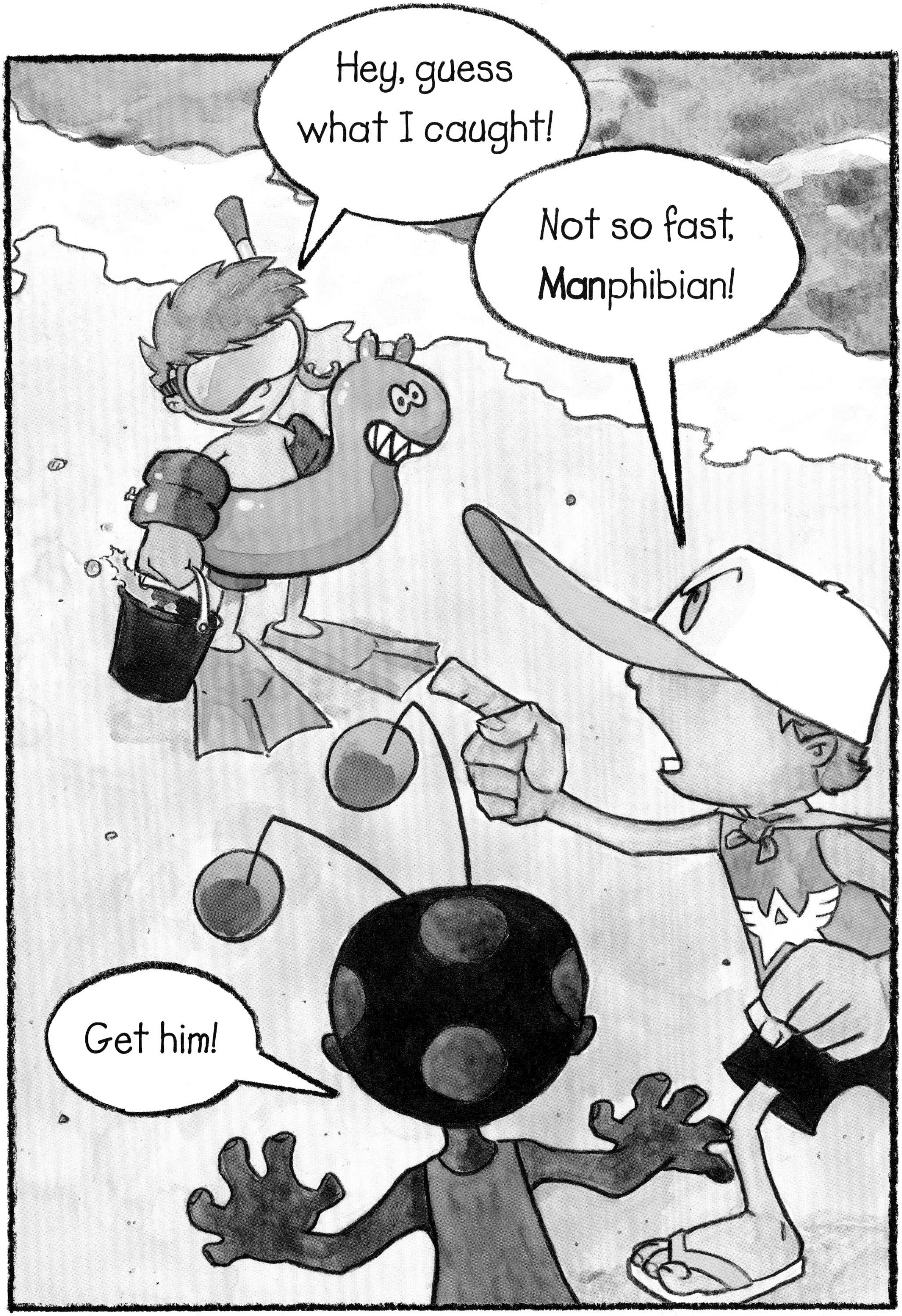
Hey, guess what I caught!
Not so fast, **Man**phibian!
Get him!

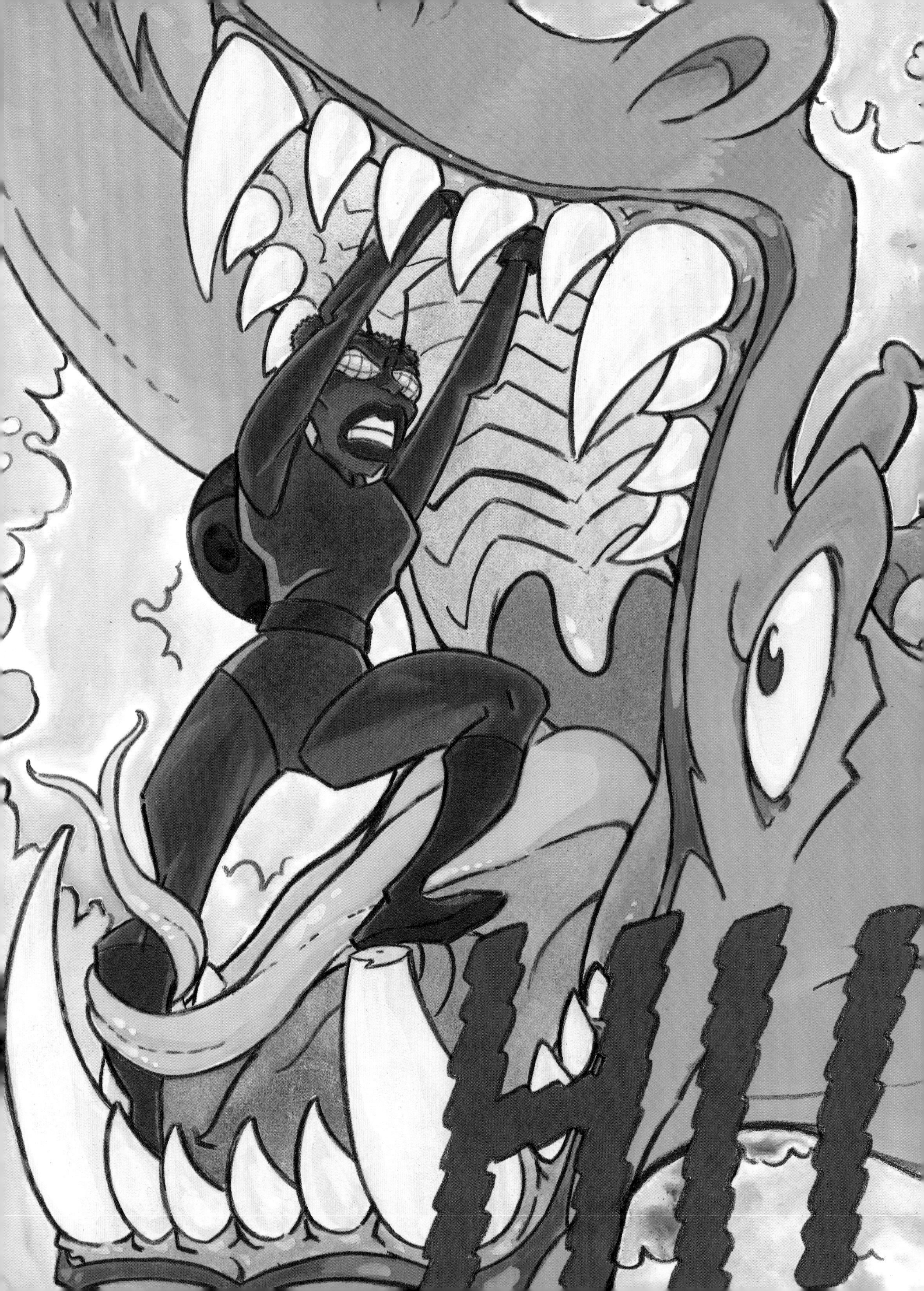
HII

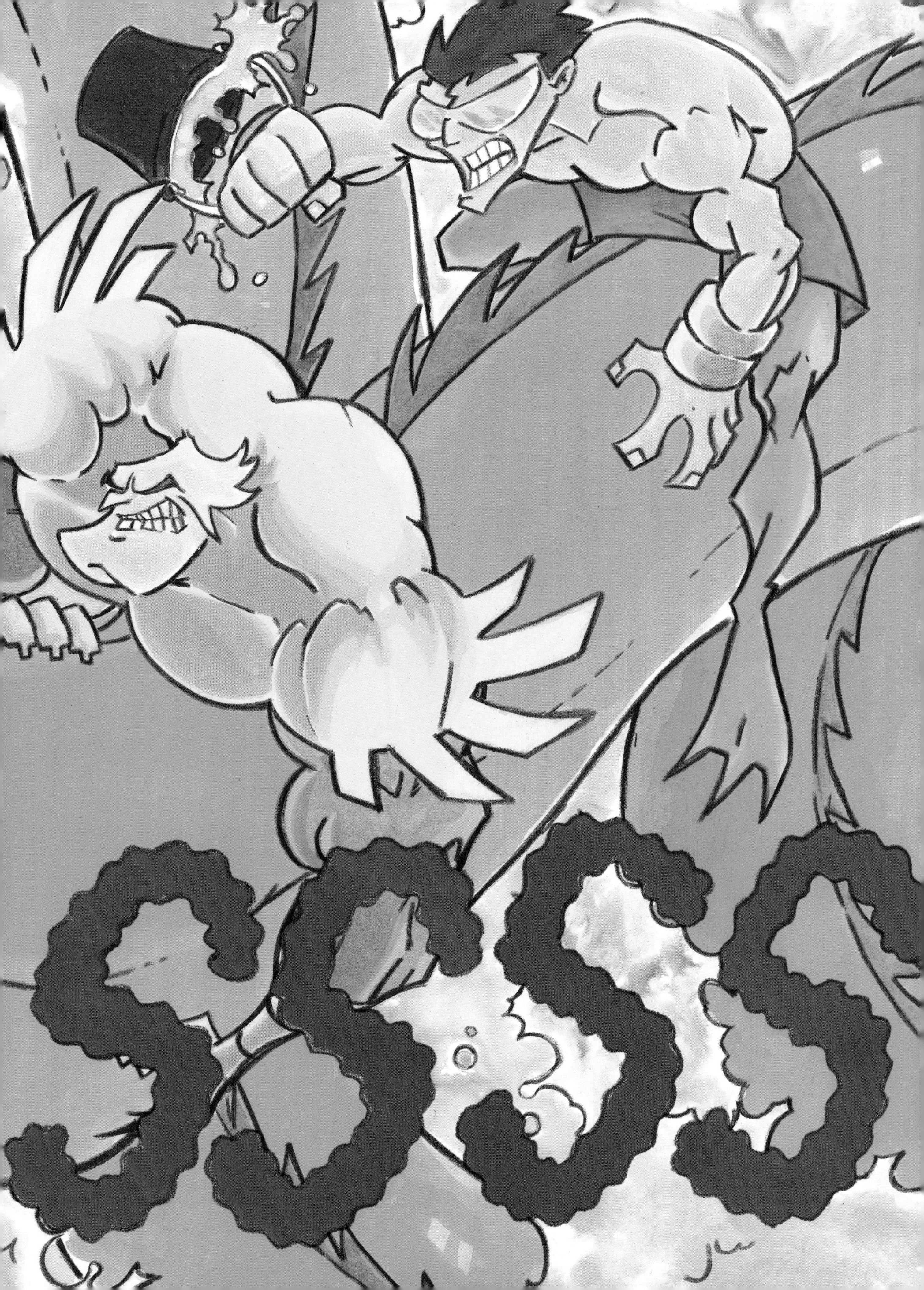
SSSS

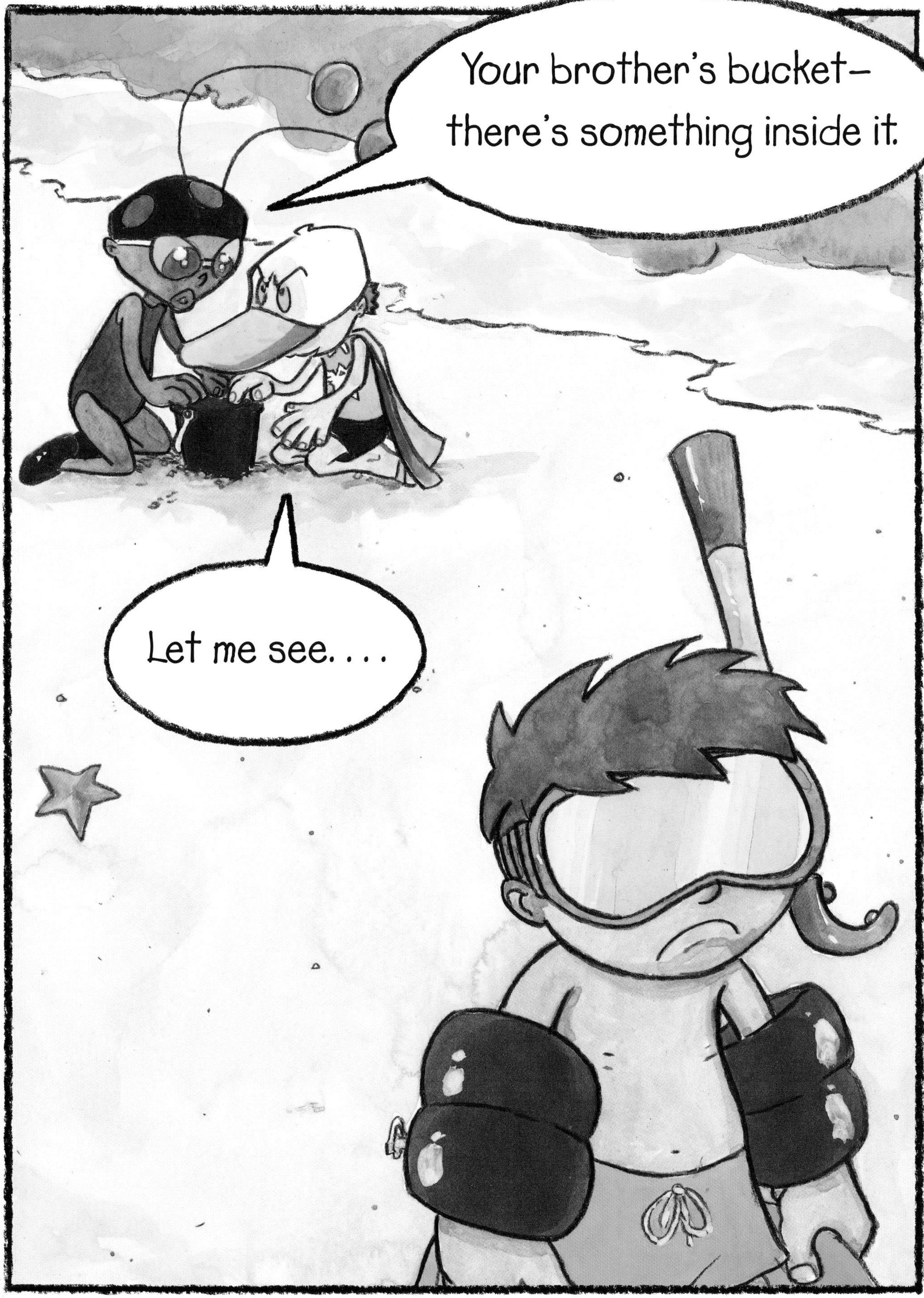
Your brother's bucket—there's something inside it.
Let me see. . . .

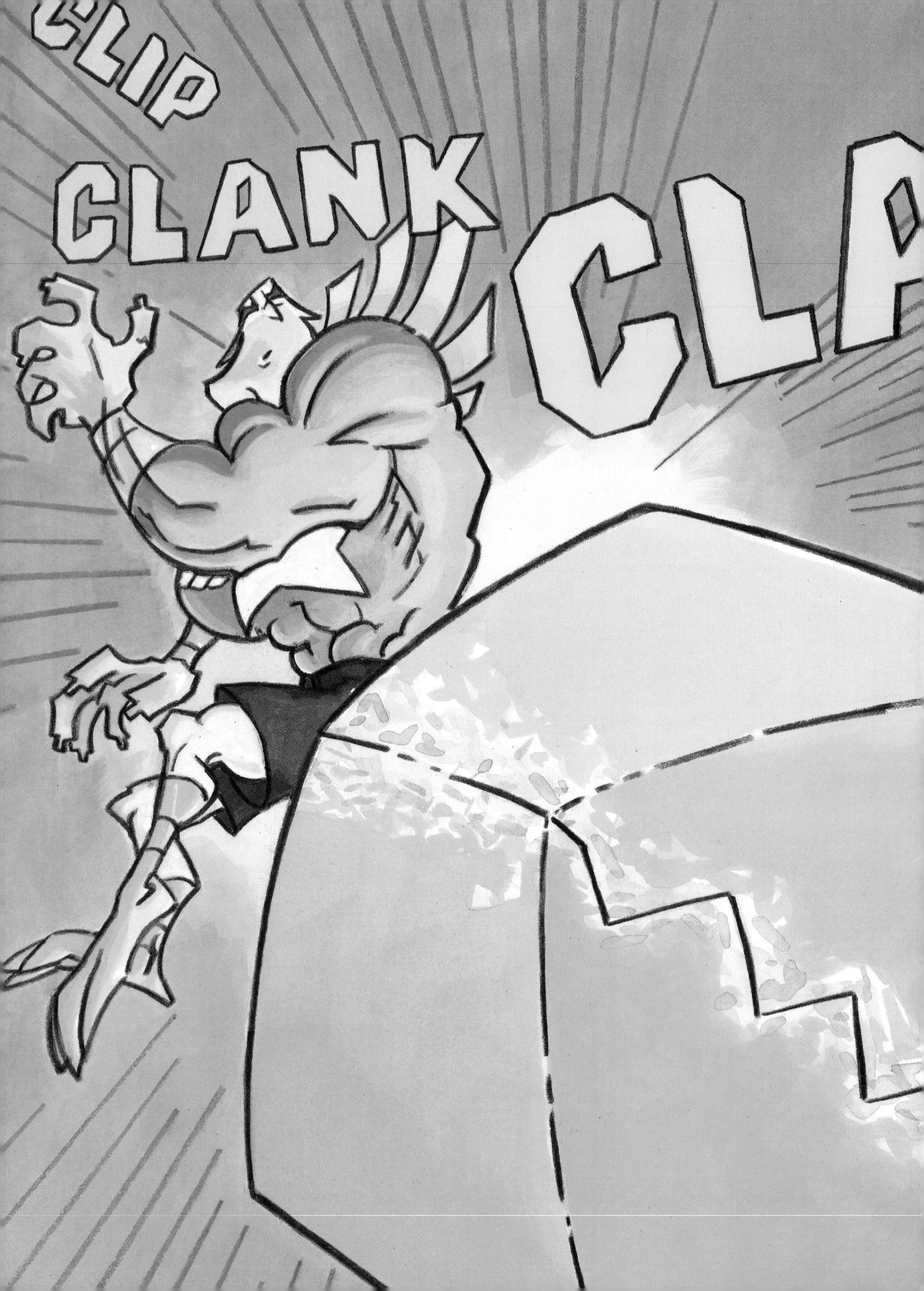
CLIP
CLANK
CLA

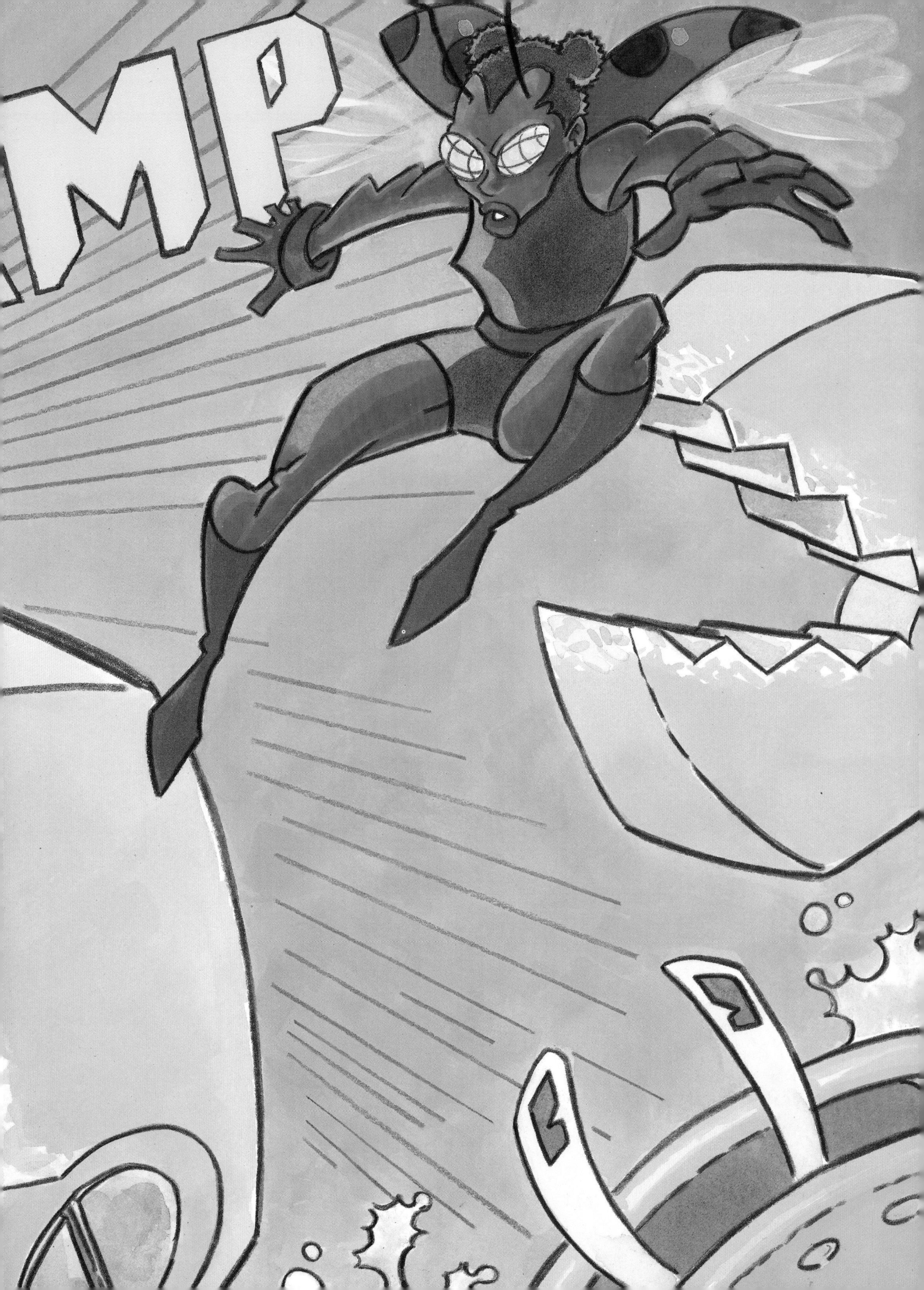
MP

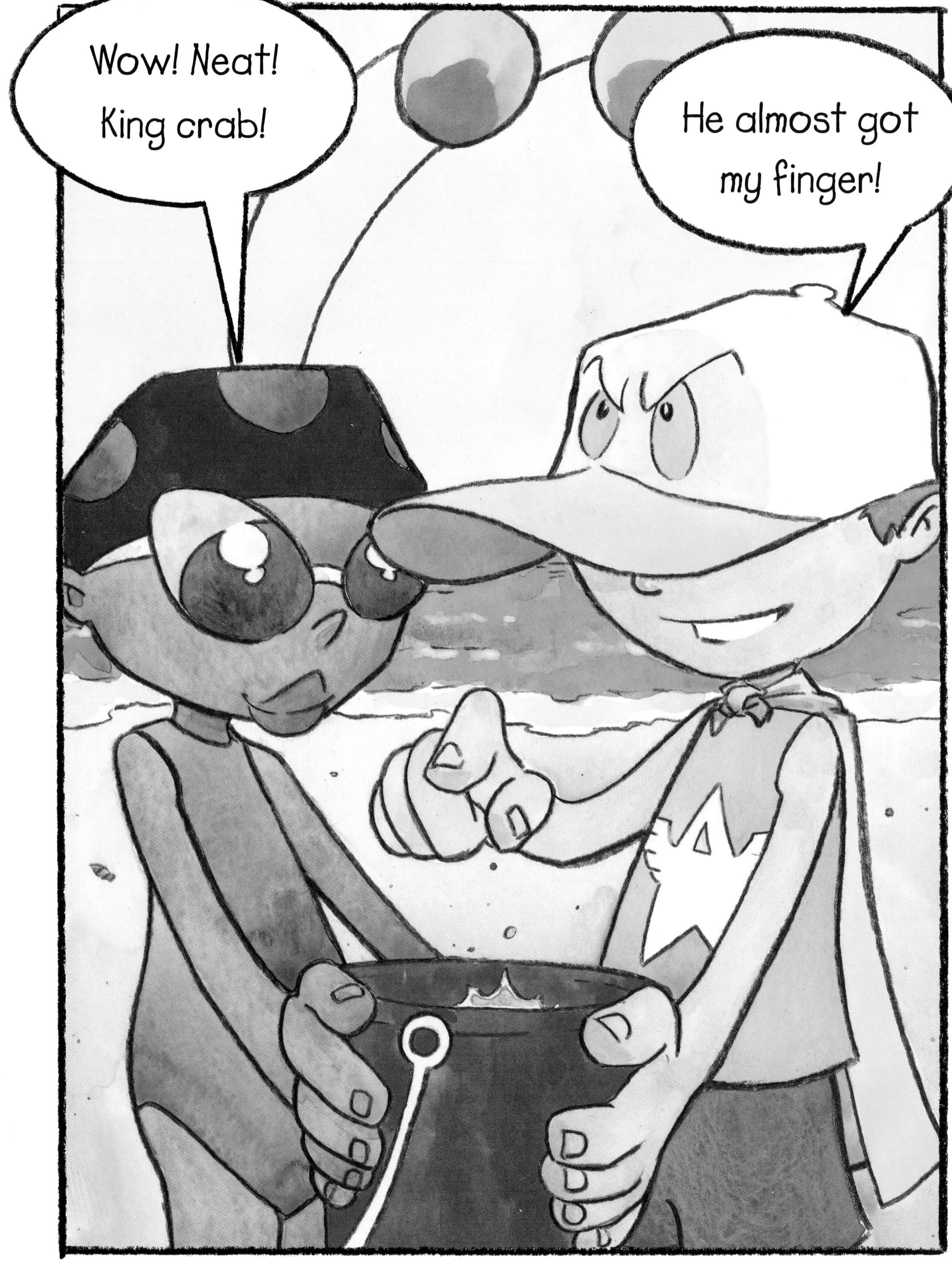
Wow! Neat! King crab!
He almost got my finger!

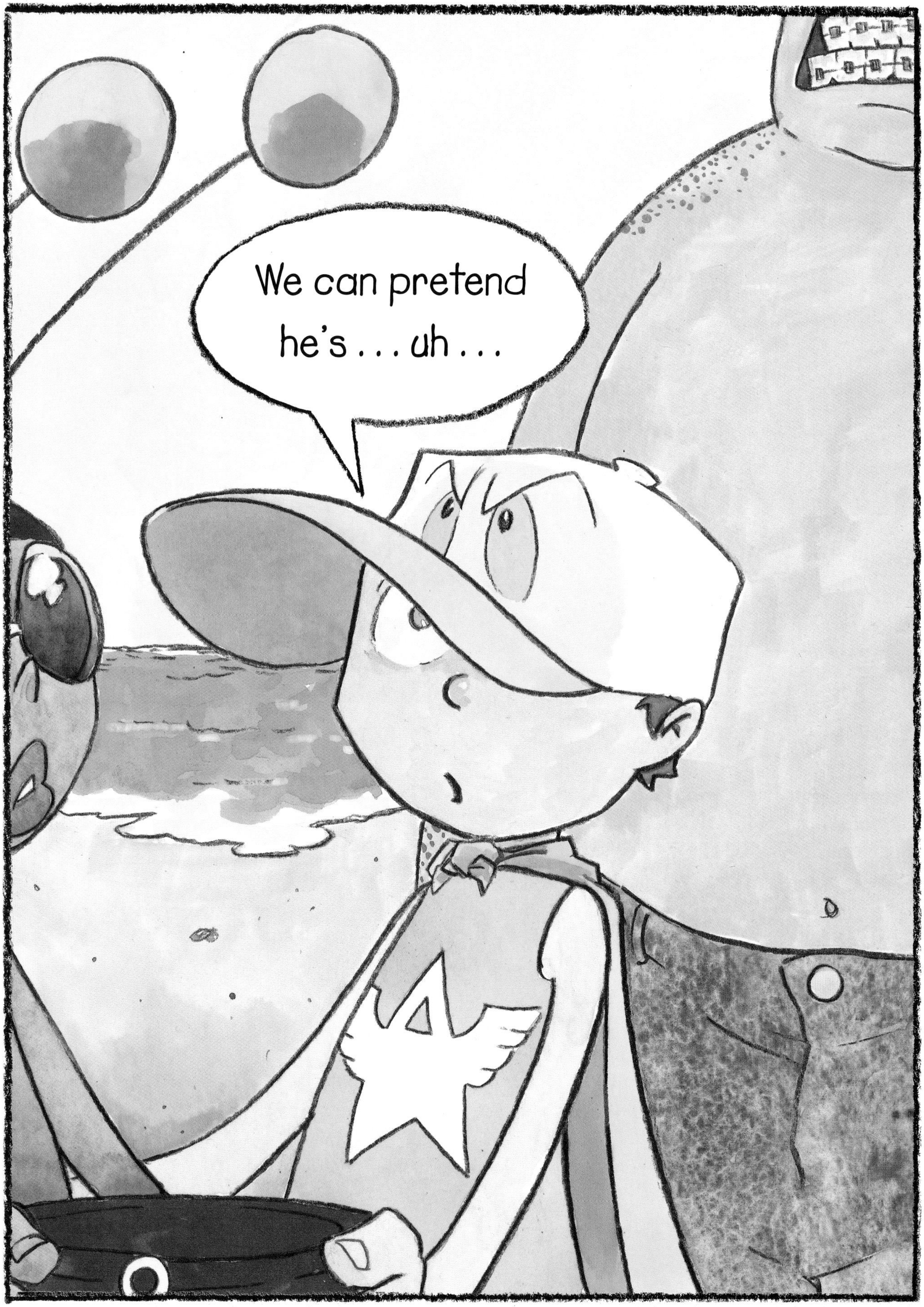
We can pretend he's . . . uh . . .

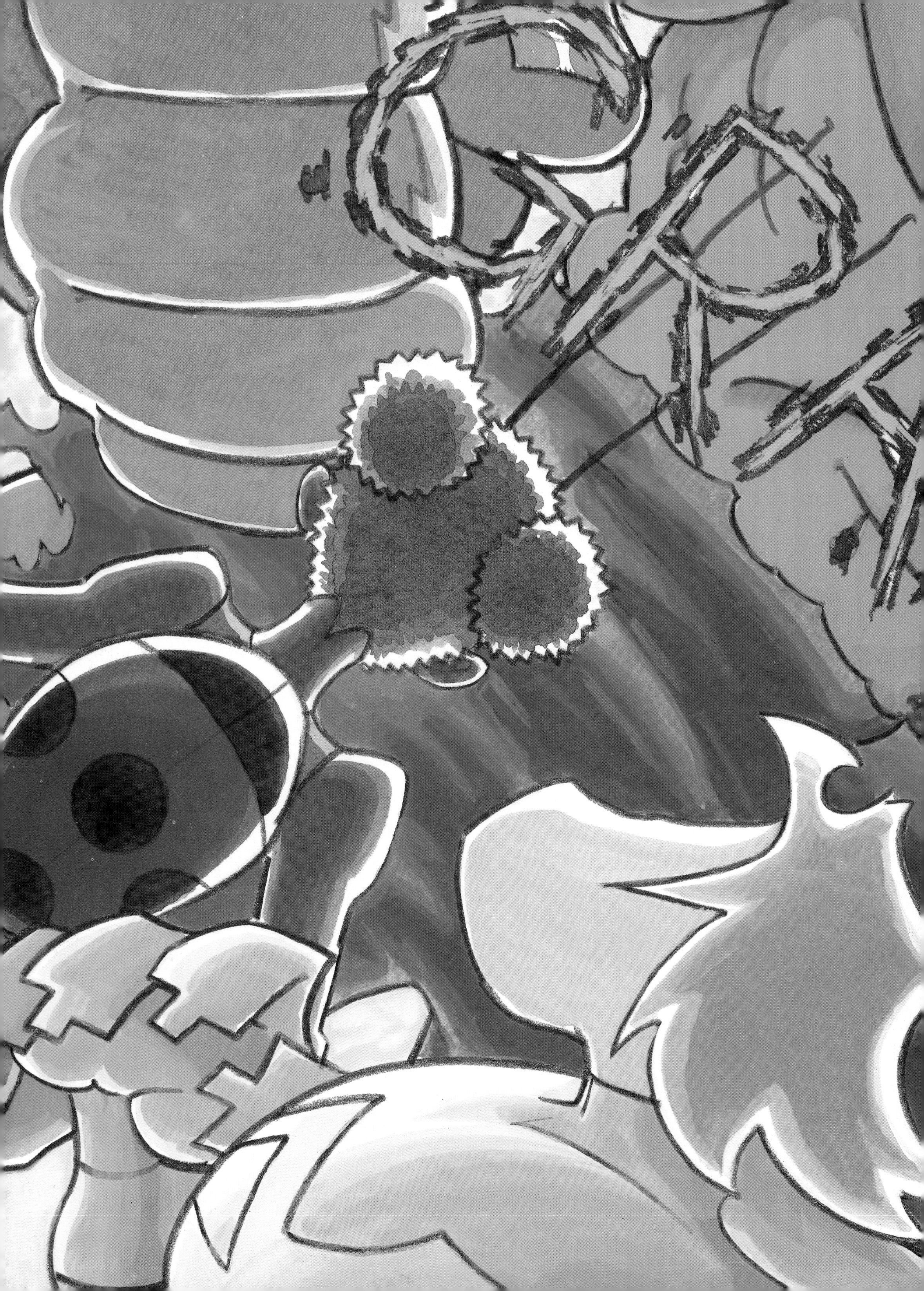

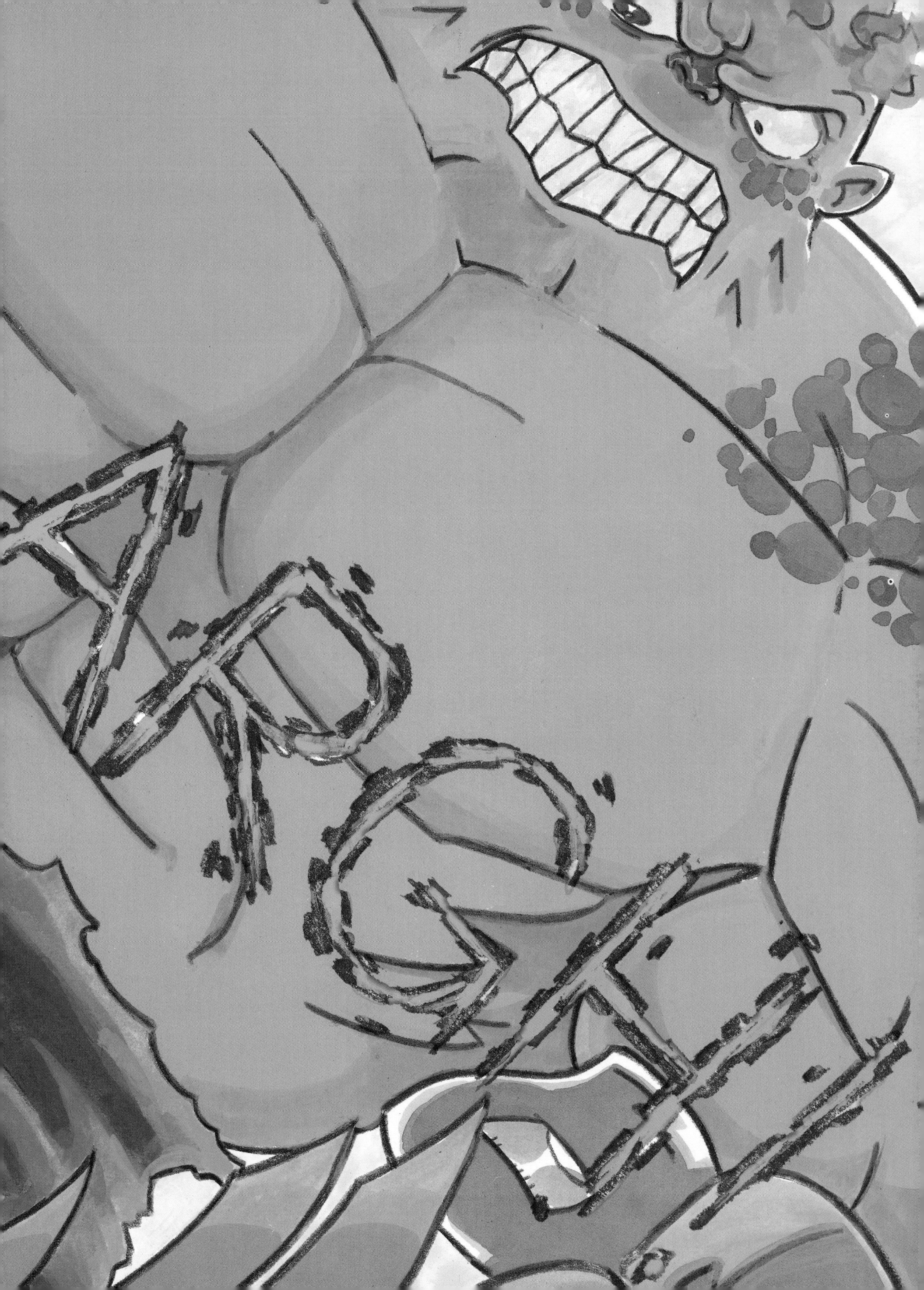
ARGH

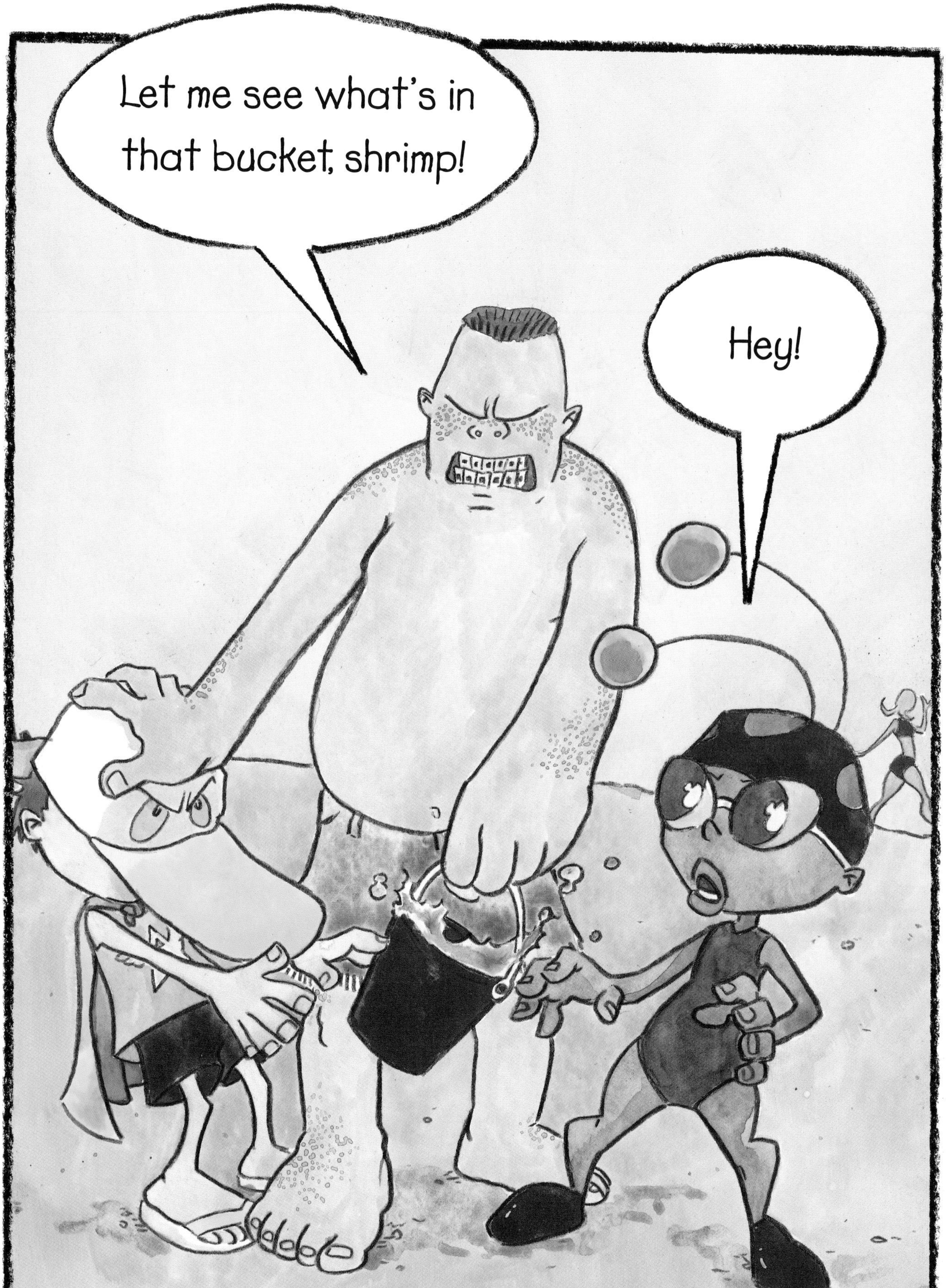
Let me see what's in that bucket, shrimp!
Hey!

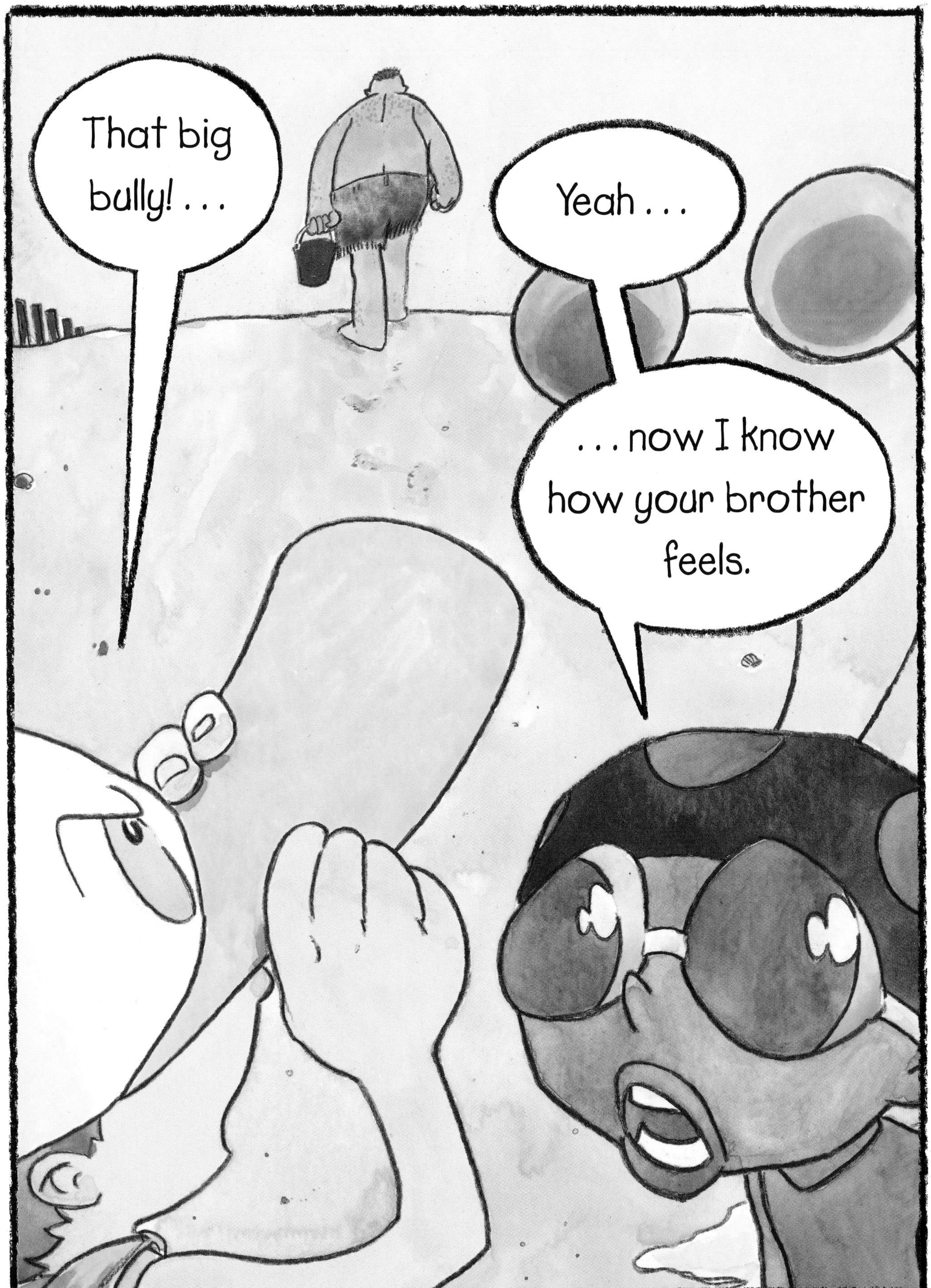
That big bully! . . .
Yeah . . .
. . . now I know how your brother feels.

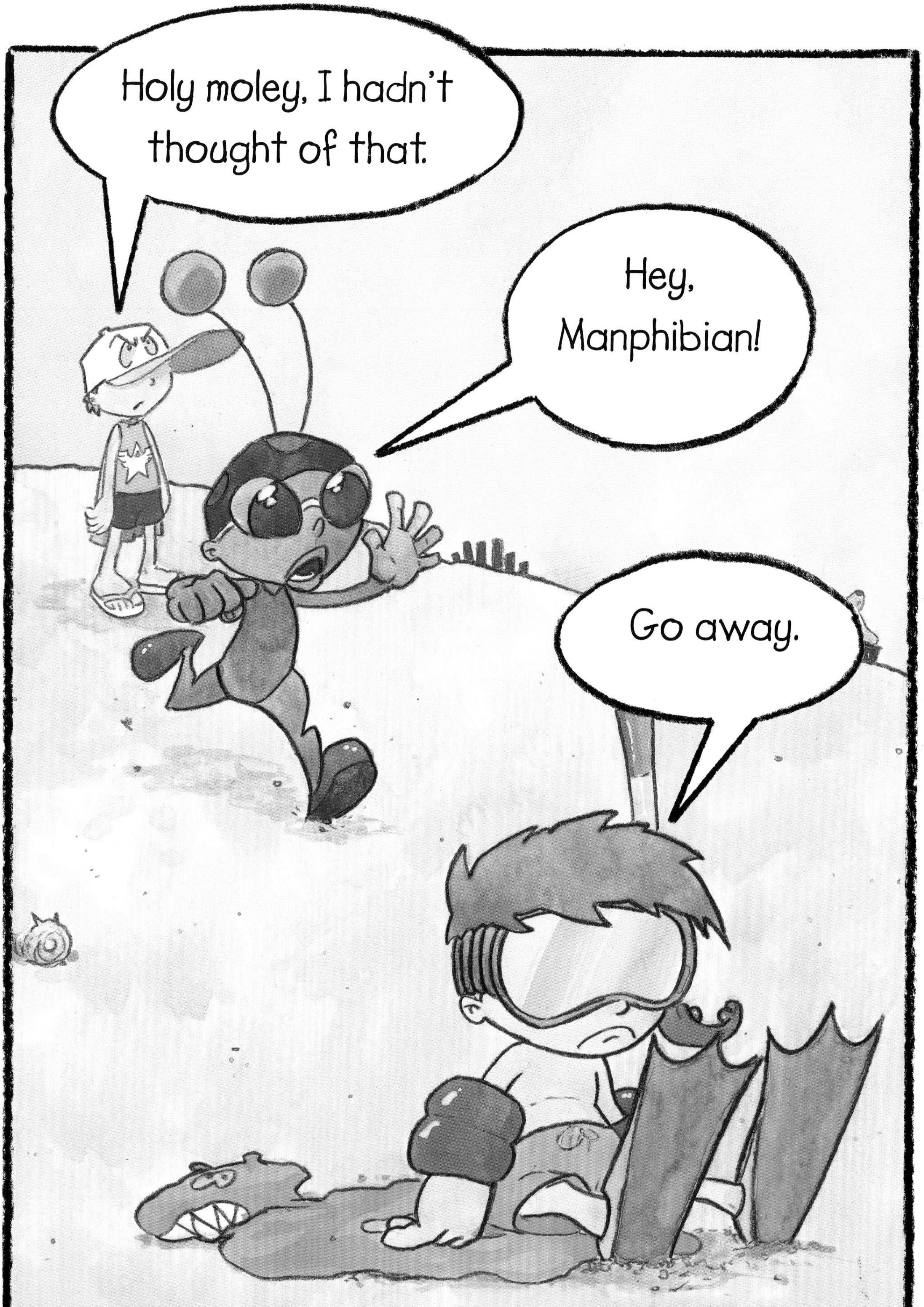
Holy moley, I hadn't thought of that.
Hey, Manphibian!
Go away.

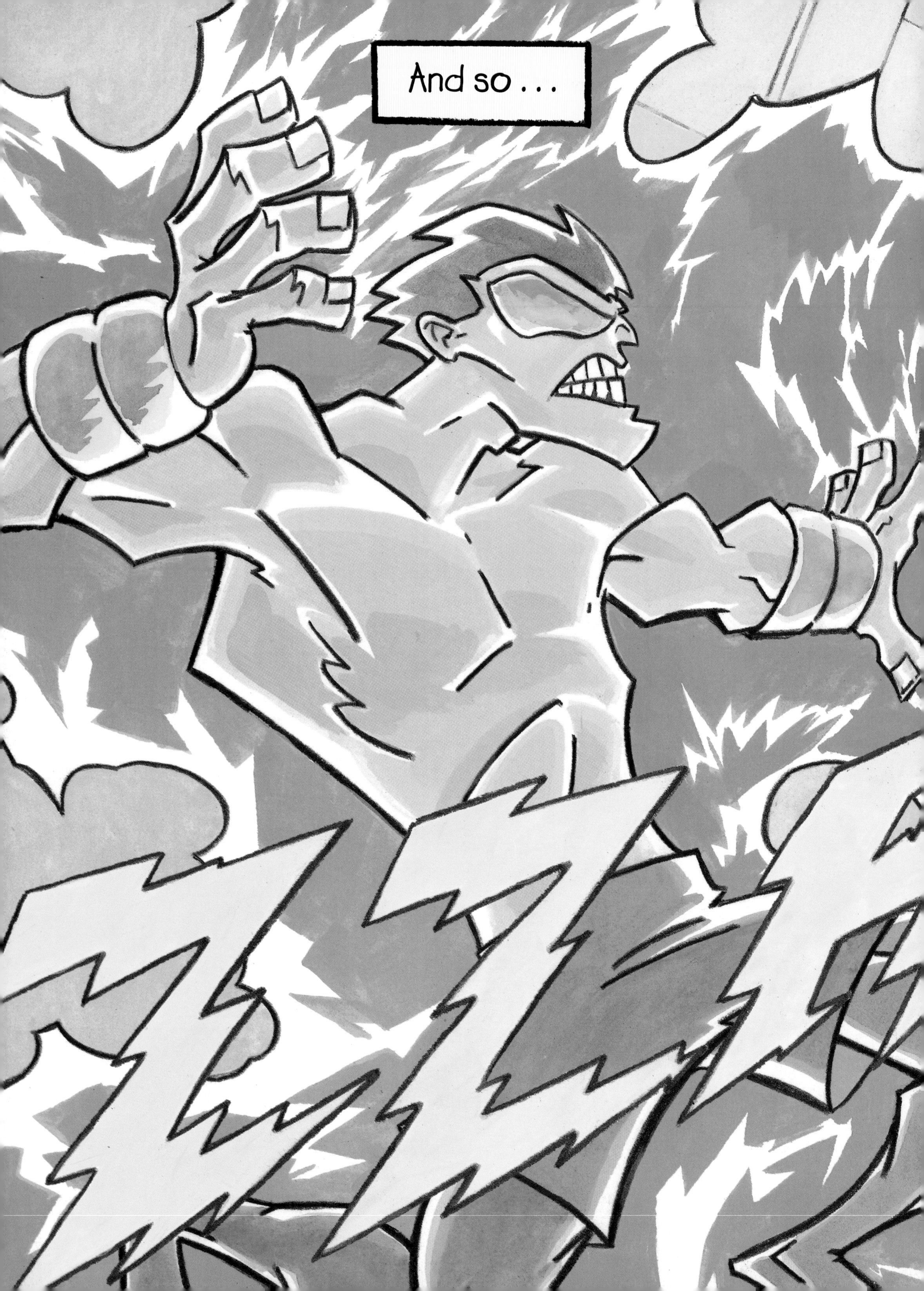
And so . . .

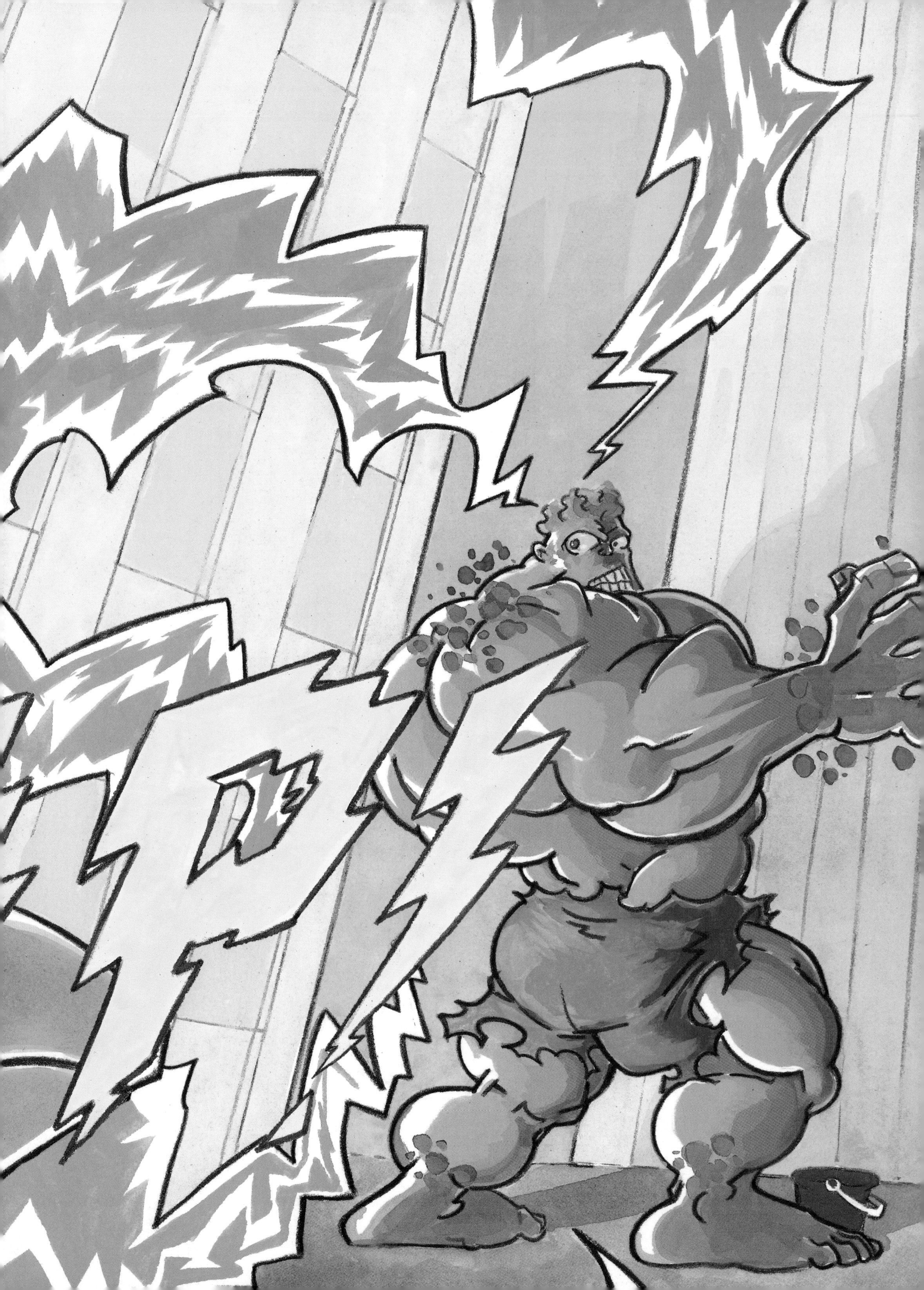

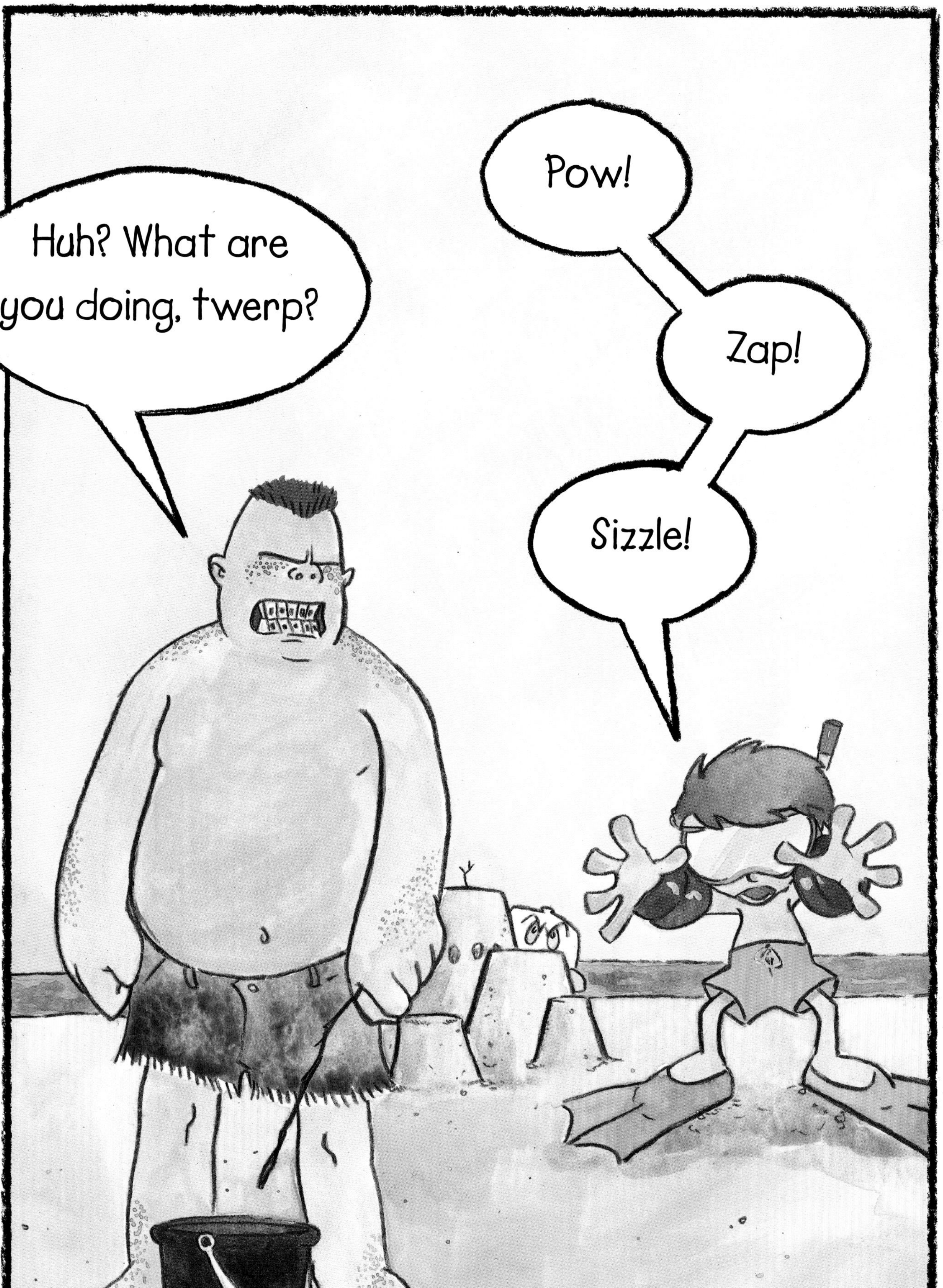
Huh? What are you doing, twerp?
Pow!
Zap!
Sizzle!

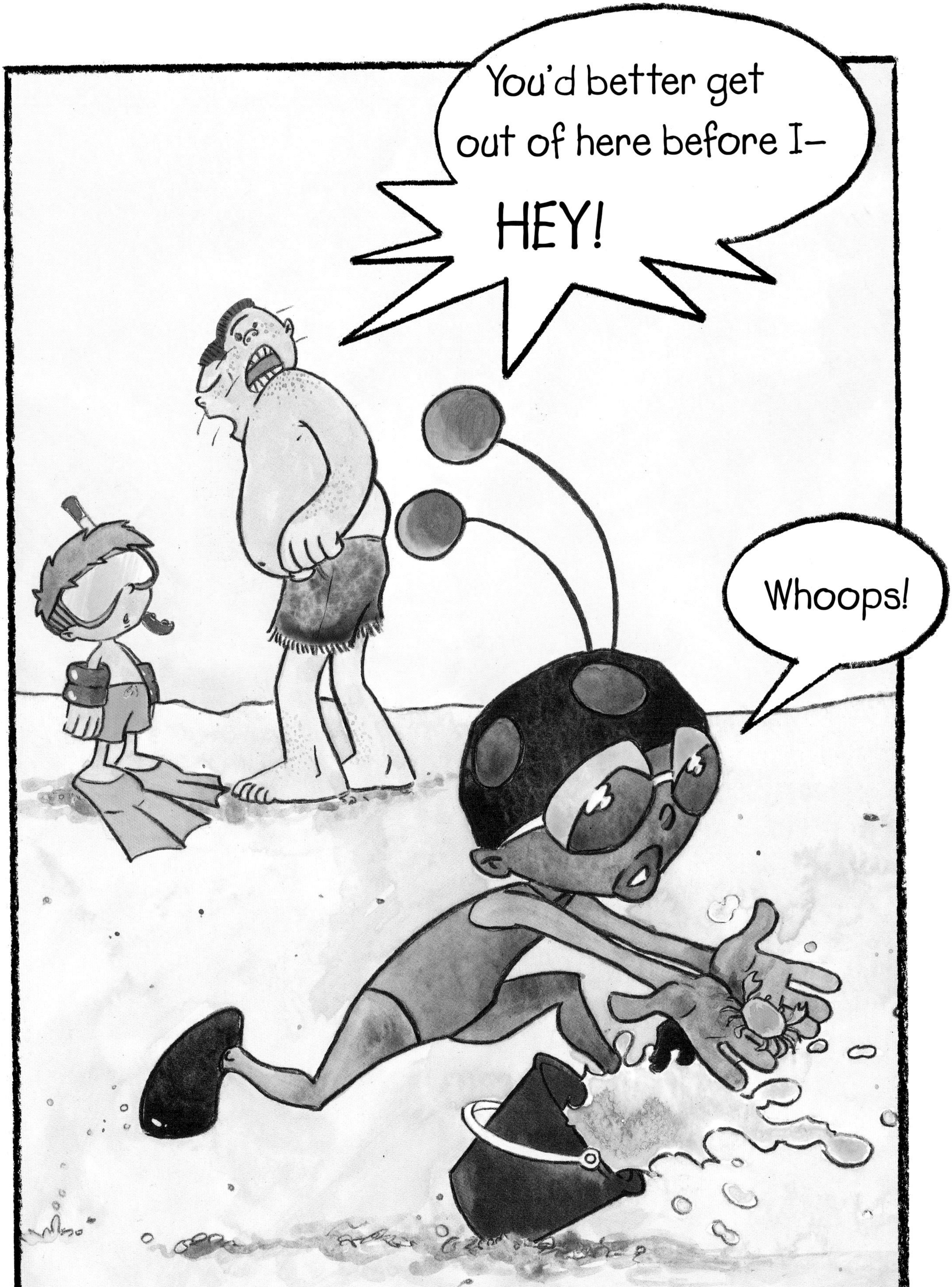
You'd better get out of here before I–
HEY!
Whoops!

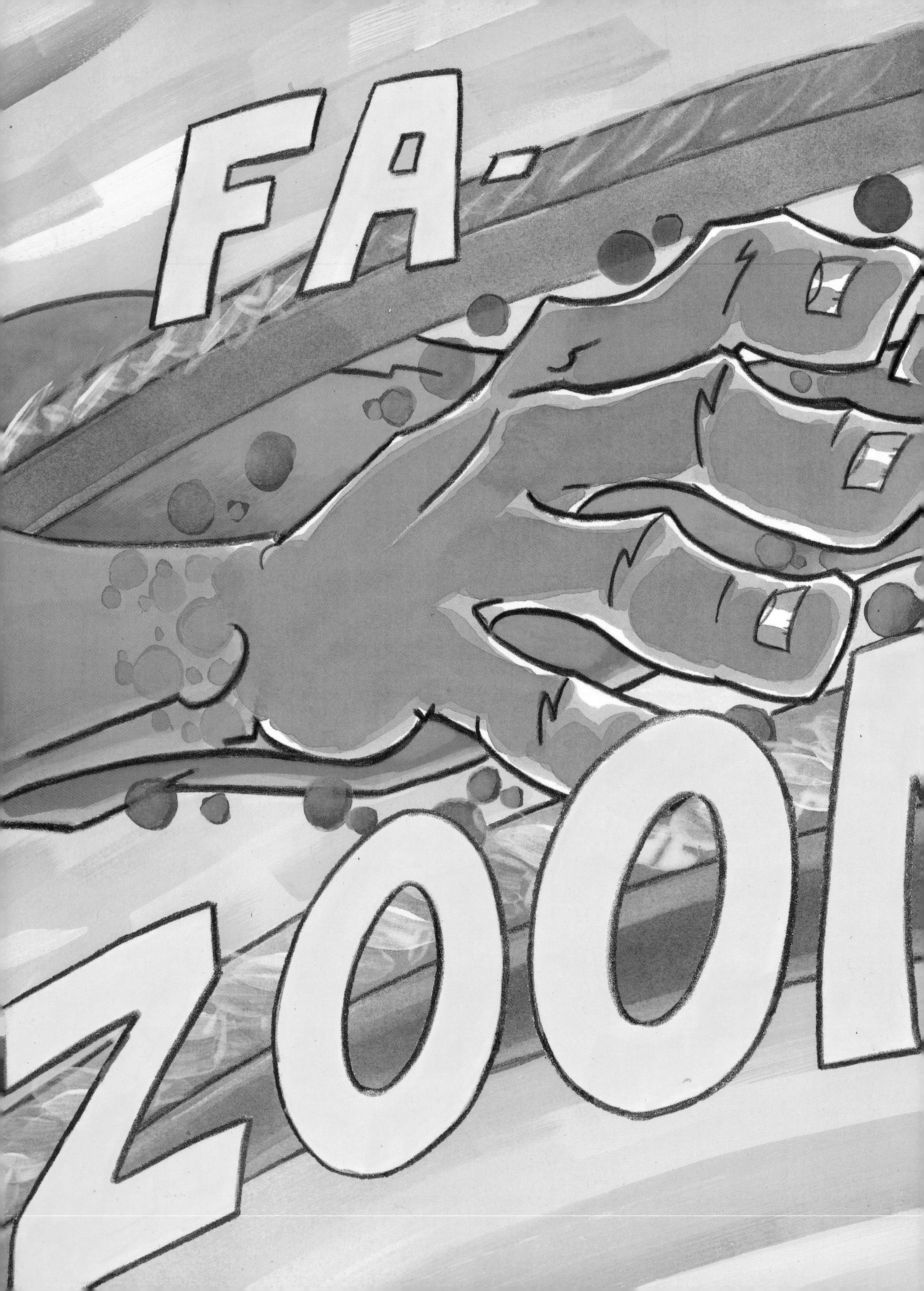
FA-
ZOO

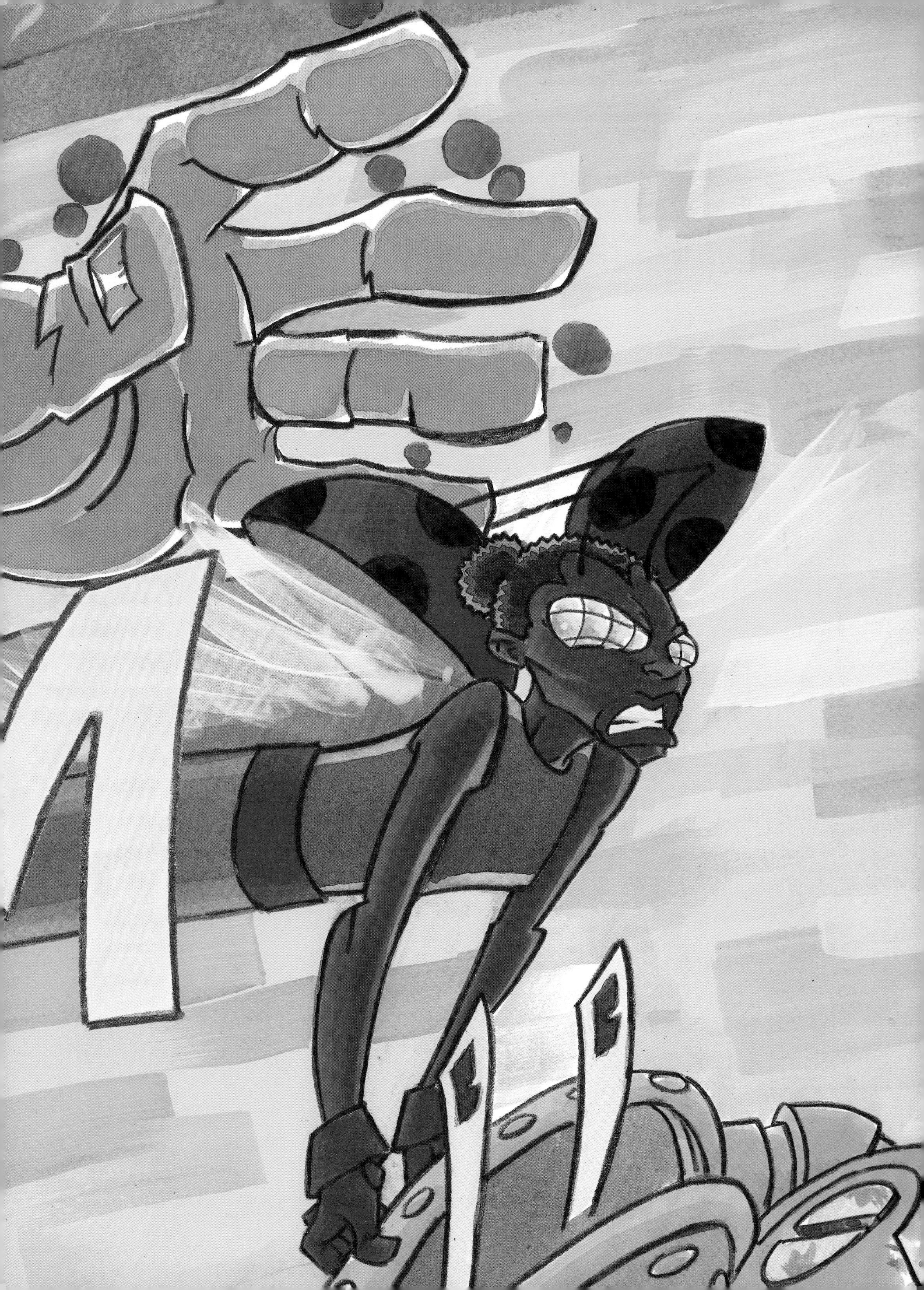

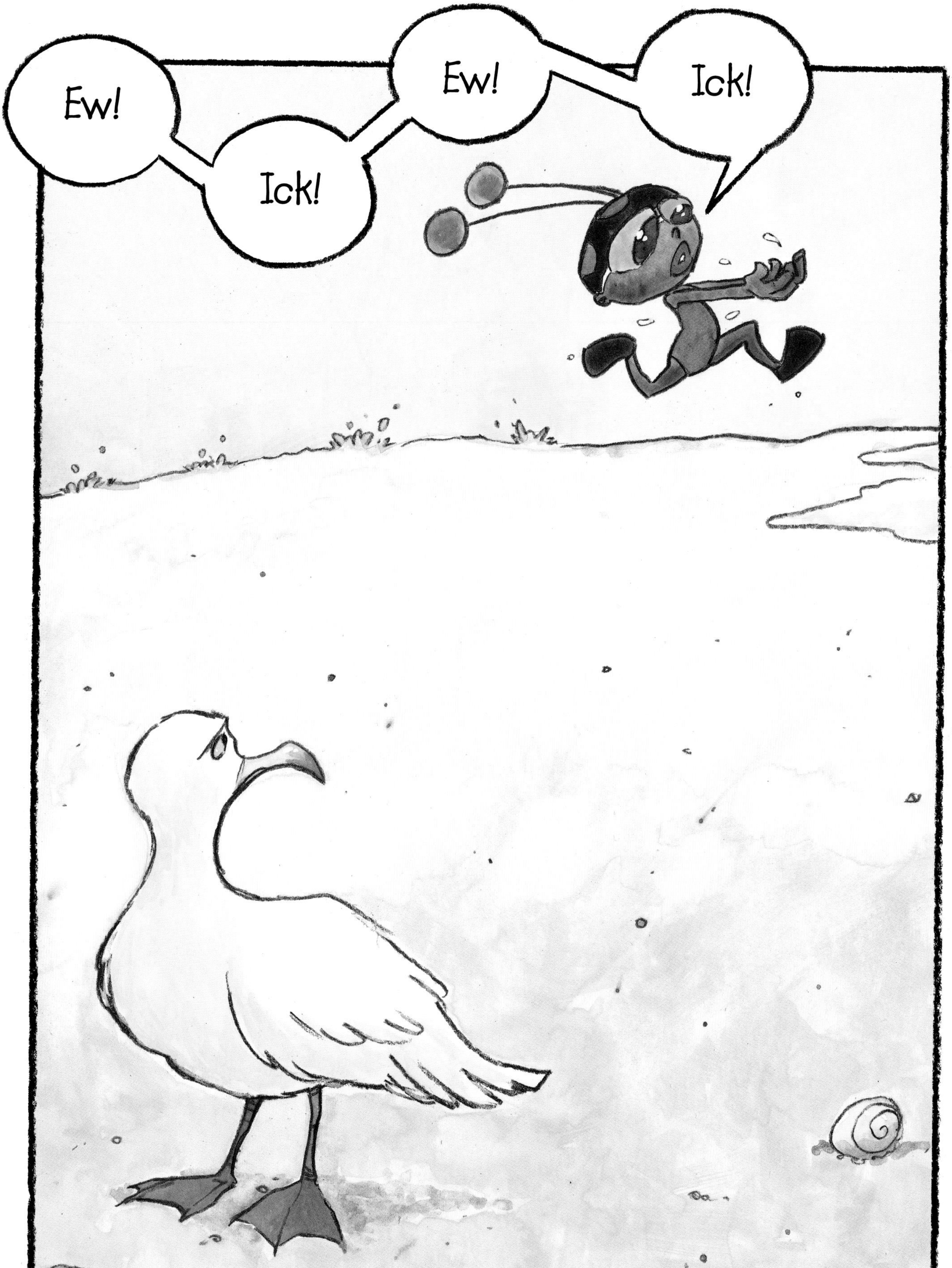
Ew!
Ick!
Ew!
Ick!

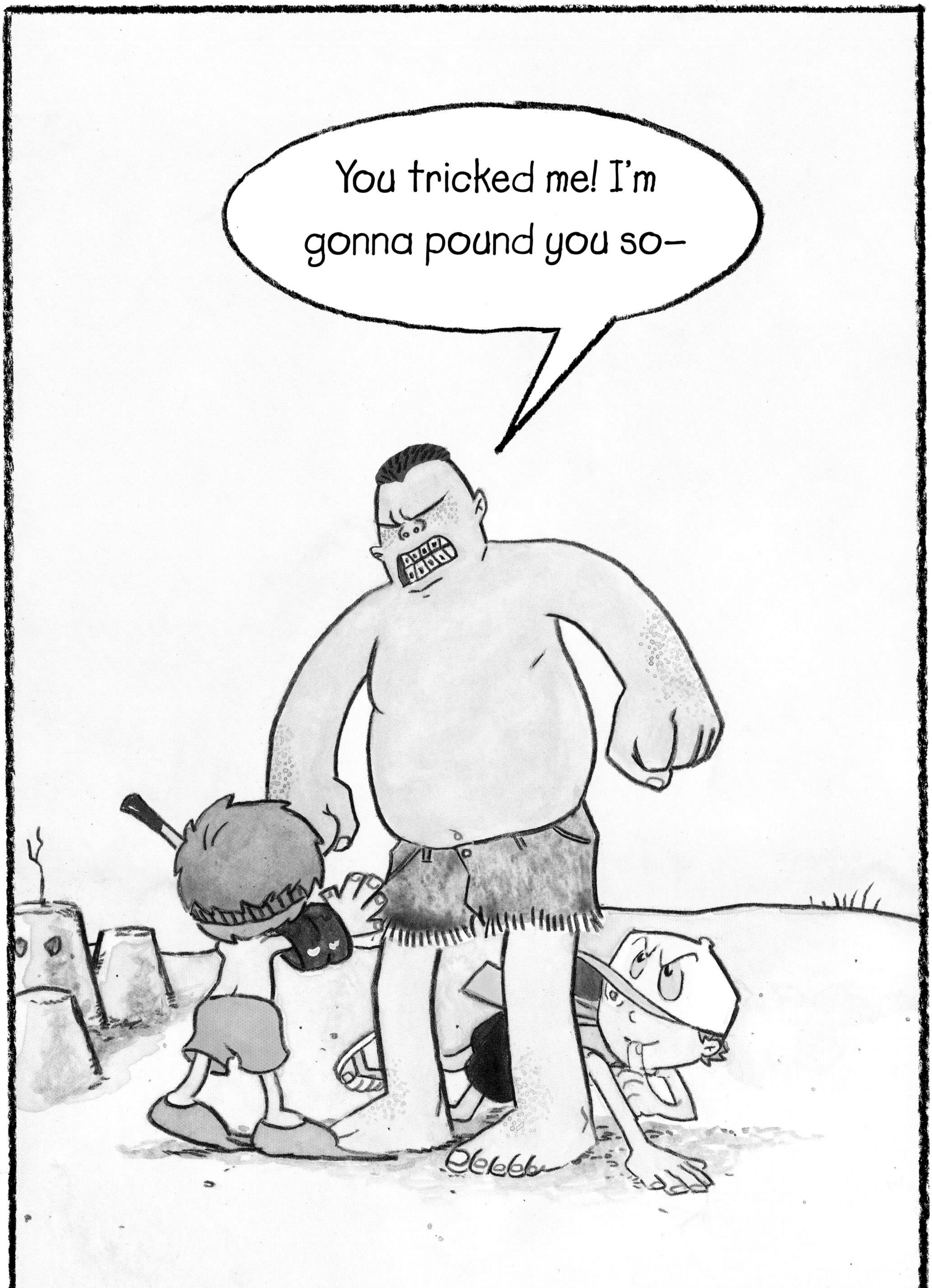
You tricked me! I'm gonna pound you so–

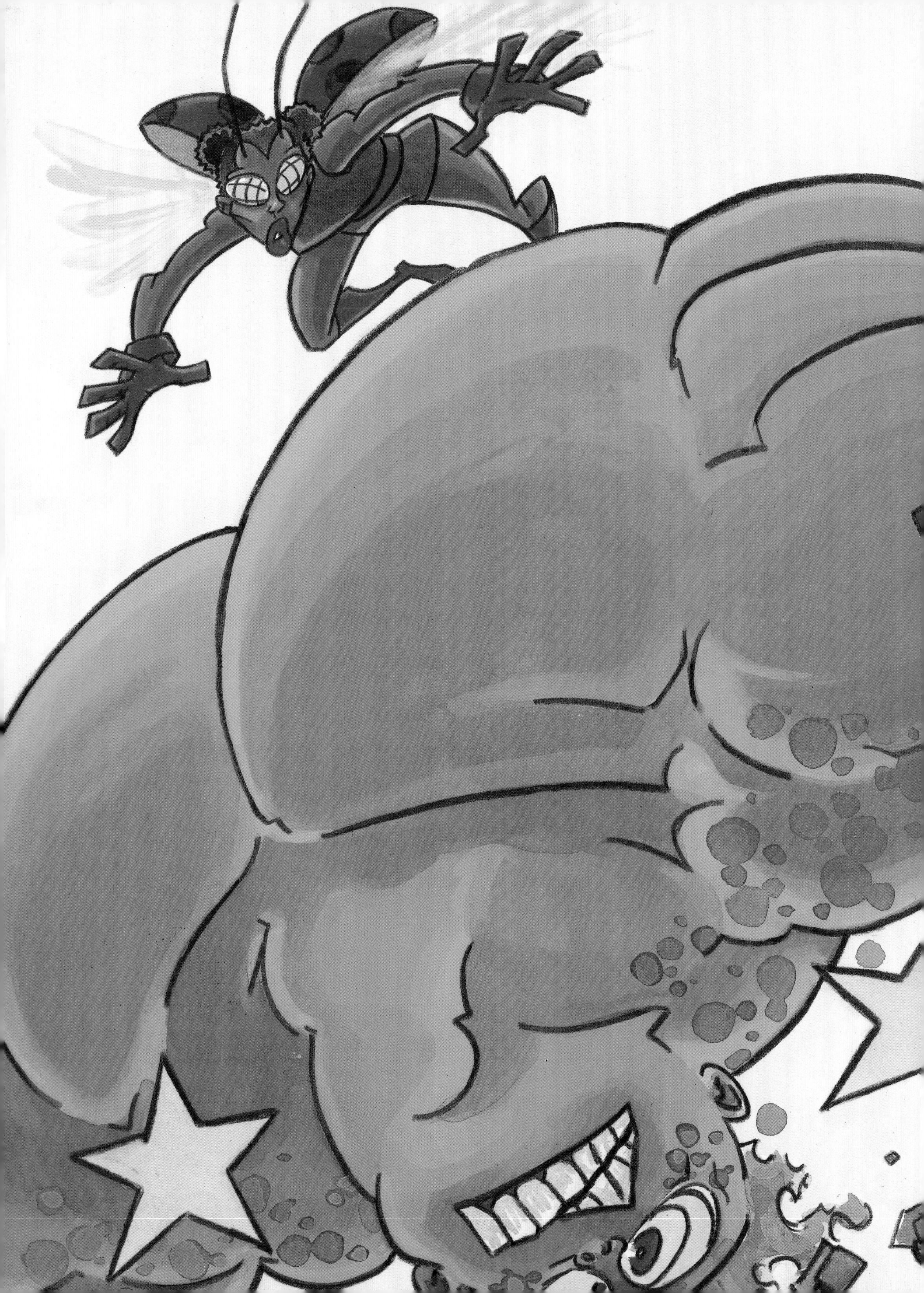

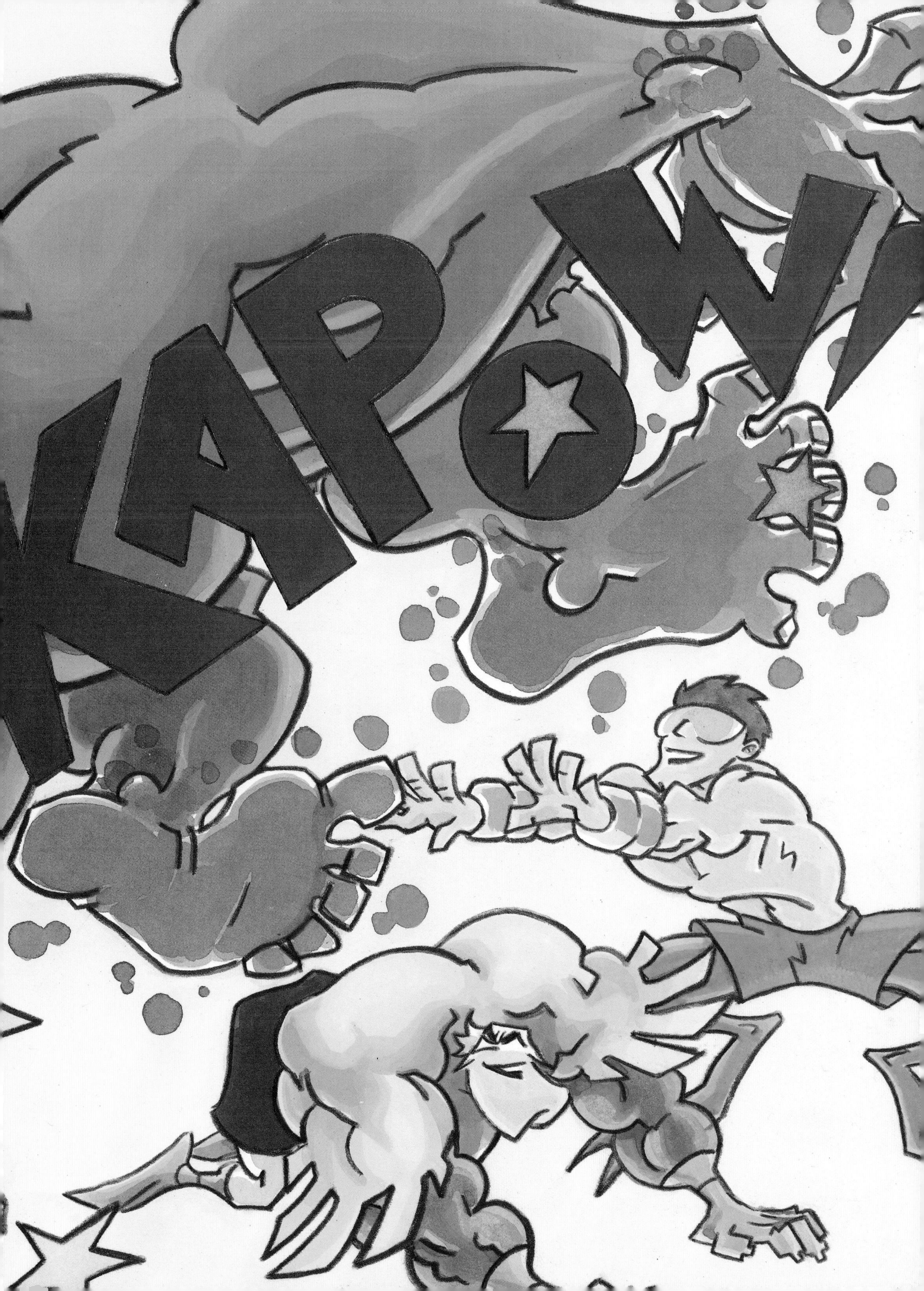
KAPOW

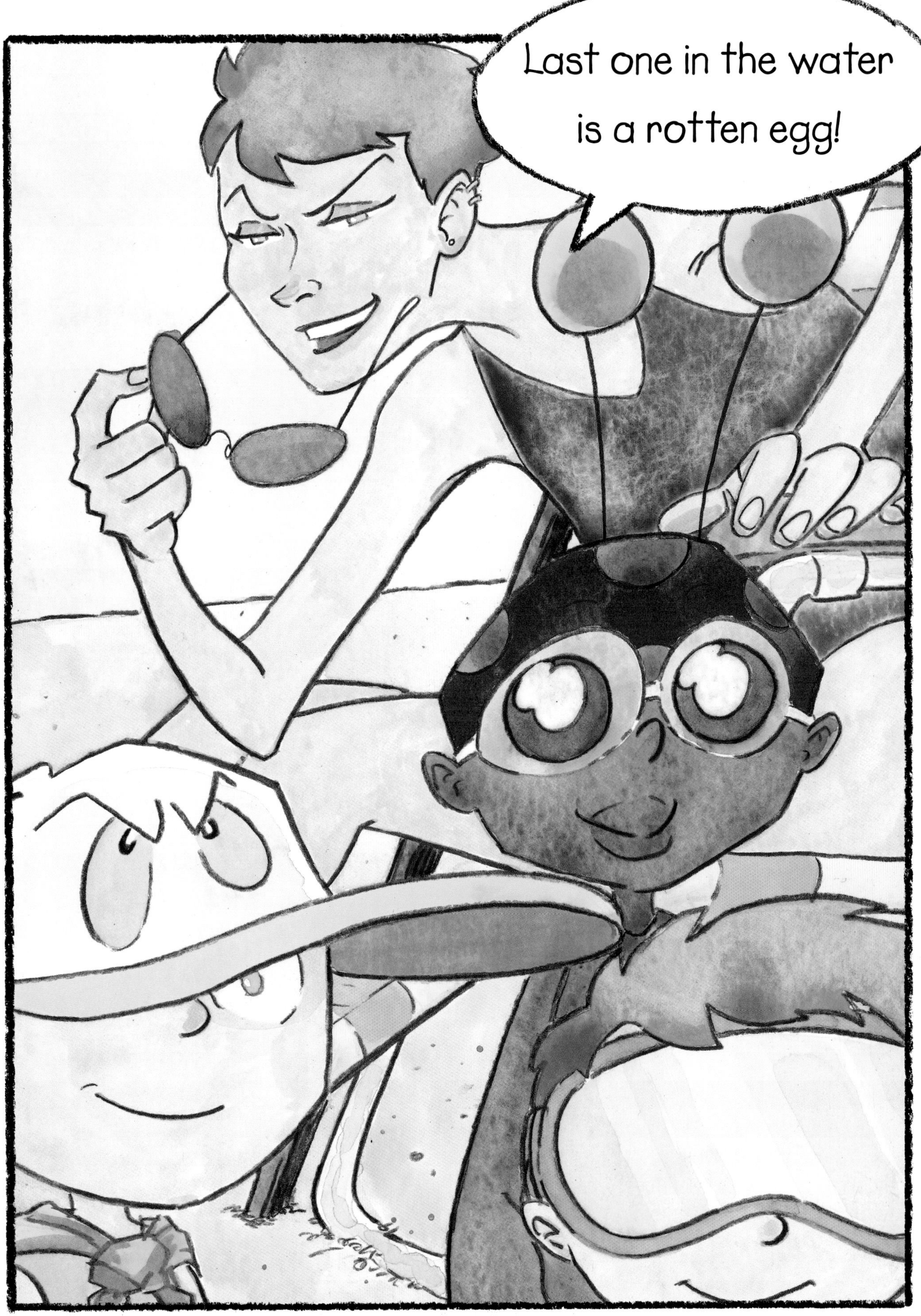
Last one in the water is a rotten egg!

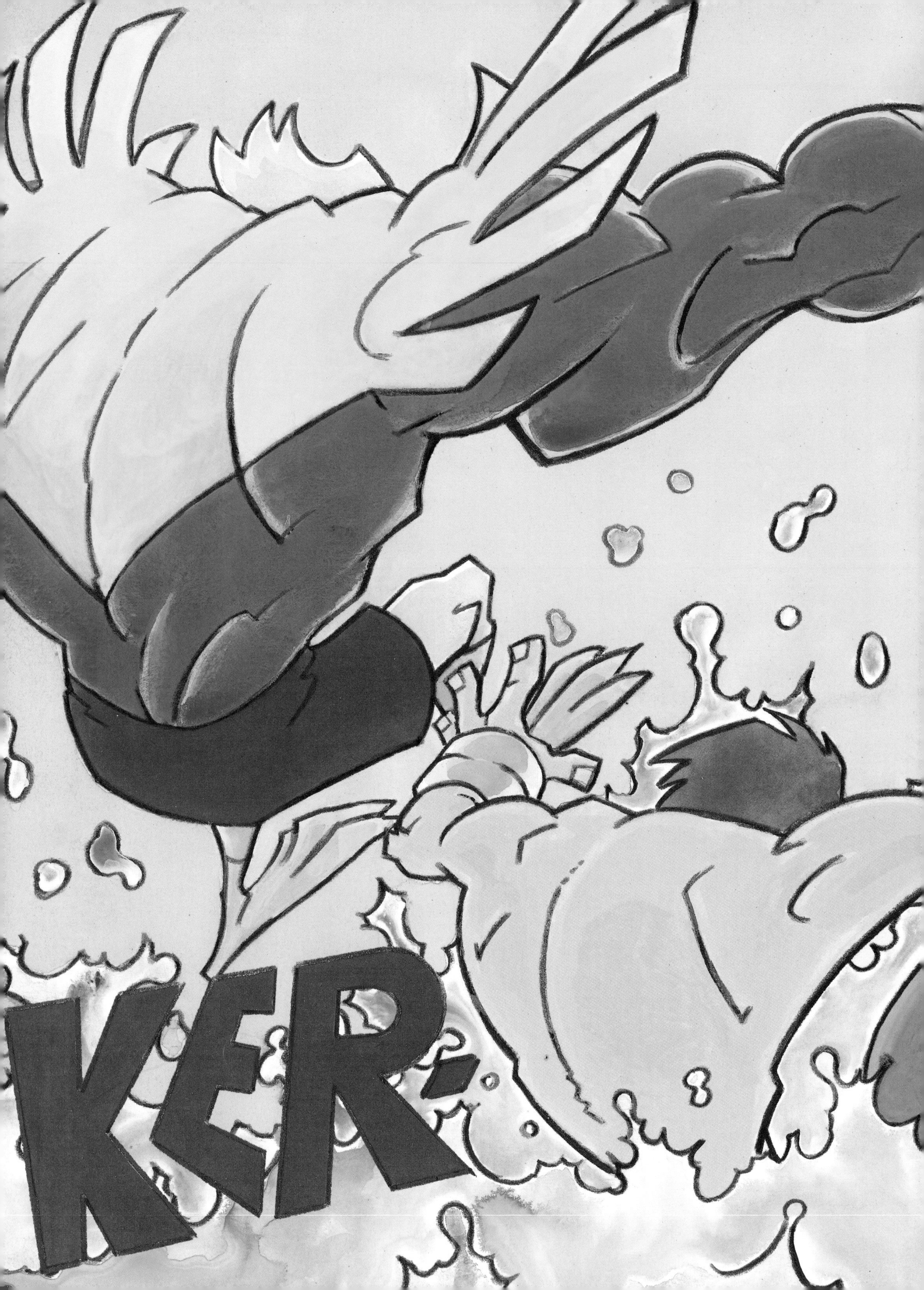
KER-

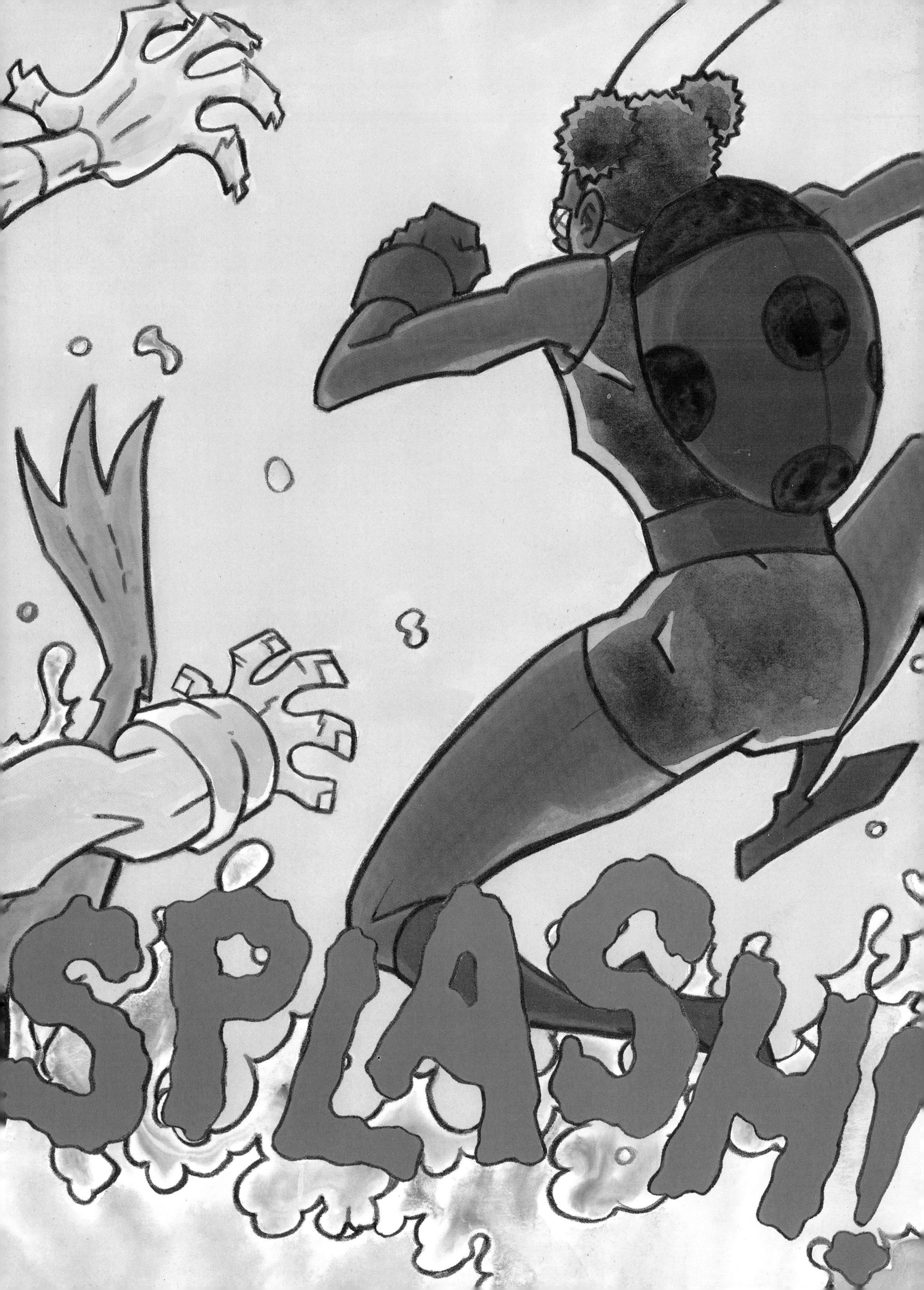
SPLASH!

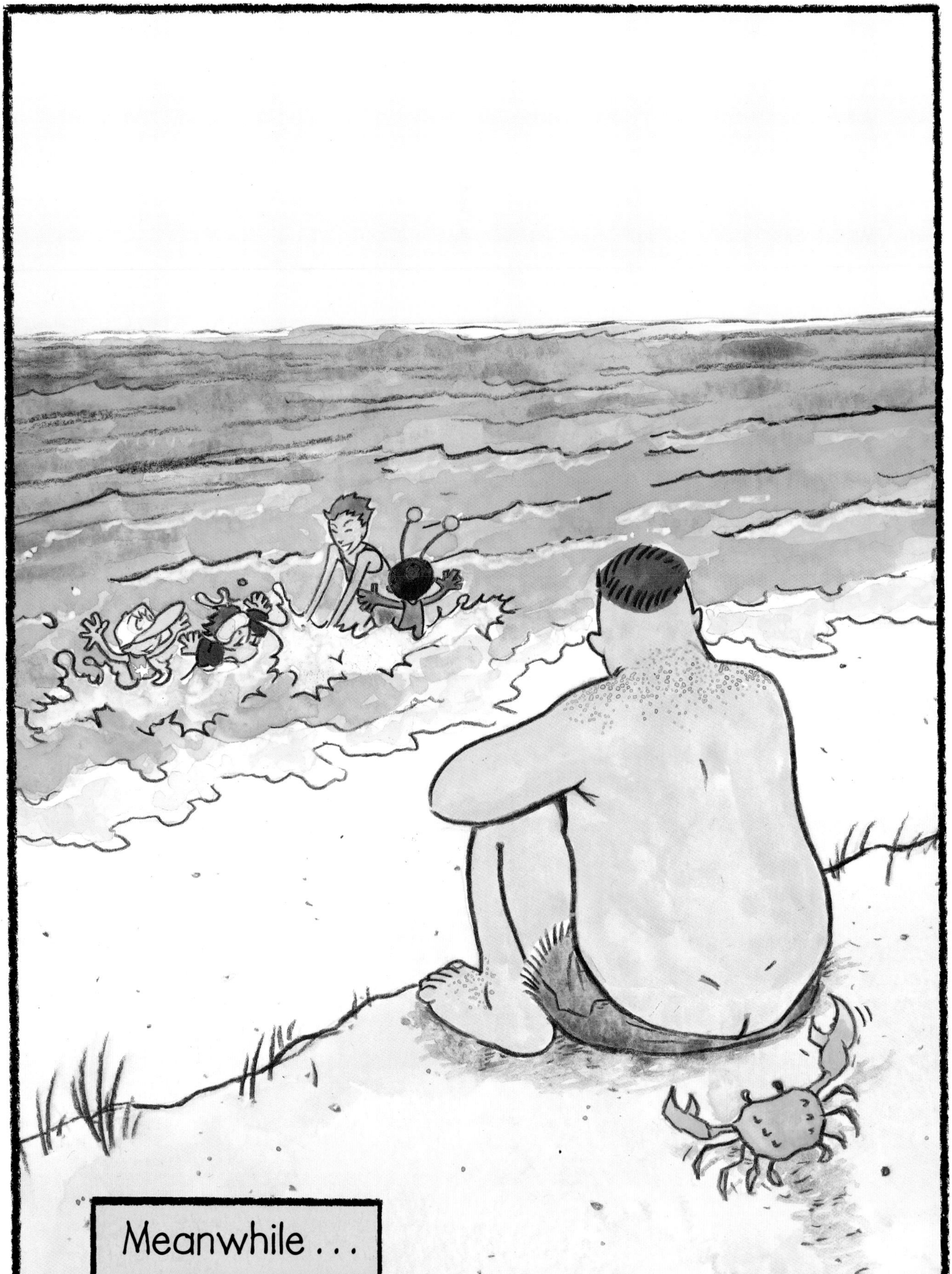
Meanwhile . . .